*Although she knew it was insanity to even consider a secret rendezvous, Pippa could not make herself say no.*

She opened her mouth to try to form the word and her lips refused. Her whole body and being wanted to be with Nic, and she was bloody tired of denying herself. "Yes," she finally said and closed her eyes. "But this could be messy."

Nic laughed. "I've been dealing with messes since I was six years old."

She wondered what it was about Nic that made her feel stronger. When she was with him, she felt as if she could do almost anything.

Pulling her slowly toward him, he gave her a dozen chances to turn away, but she didn't. She couldn't.

"Do you want me just because you can't have me?" she whispered, the fear squeezing out of her throat.

"No," he said. "Besides, we both know I can and will have you. The question is when," he said and lowered his mouth to hers.

Dear Reader,

This is one of my most ambitious books ever! These characters got inside my head and heart and demanded that I deal with subject matter I've never attempted before. In my mind, there are two she-ros in this book, but don't worry! Only one of them is the "romantic lead." And what a woman she is. A shy bookworm princess with bad hair who is known for not making waves is thrust into a situation that challenges her to be stronger than she ever dreamed she could be.

The second she-ro is the hero's mother. I pictured her as an older but still gamin Audrey Hepburn determined to savor every moment of life. The dreamy forbidden hero comes from a long line of pirates. I see Nic Lafitte looking like a slightly rougher-edged version of Antonio Sabato, Jr. I love the way shy Princess Pippa turns worldly Nic's head and heart around in ways he would have considered impossible.

Throw in a long-standing family feud and a crowd of Royals, and our hero and she-ro are in for the journey of their lives. I hope this story will be a "heart-warmer" for you….

Wishing you love and joy,

Leanne

# THE PRINCESS
# AND THE
# OUTLAW

## *LEANNE BANKS*

entertain, enrich, inspire™

Recycling programs
for this product may
not exist in your area.

ISBN-13: 978-0-373-65680-6

THE PRINCESS AND THE OUTLAW

---

## LEANNE BANKS

is a *New York Times* and *USA TODAY* bestselling author who is surprised every time she realizes how many books she has written. Leanne loves chocolate, the beach and new adventures. To name a few, Leanne has ridden on an elephant, stood on an ostrich egg (no, it didn't break), gone parasailing and indoor skydiving. Leanne loves writing romance because she believes in the power and magic of love. She lives in Virginia with her family and a four-and-a-half-pound Pomeranian named Bijou. Visit her website, www.leannebanks.com.

This is dedicated to the family members and friends who hang in there for the long haul when a loved one is terminally ill. May the special people in your life who have passed on continue to inspire you, make you laugh, make you wise and make you love forever....

## *Prologue*

"**W**hat is *he* doing here?"

Phillipa was wondering the same thing. At her sister Bridget's gasp, her other sister, Tina, leaned toward Bridget. "Zach says he's a huge contributor here. Everyone loves him," Tina said distastefully.

"They clearly don't know him," Bridget said and nudged Phillipa. "Why can't we escape him?" she whispered. "Maybe it's because he's the devil and that means he can be everywhere at once."

At that moment, Phillipa almost agreed with Bridget. Nic certainly seemed to have some kind of dark power over her.

Phillipa had tried to slow things down with Nic Lafitte, but persuading the man to move at anything other than warp speed had proven impossible. He was a force of nature with a will that rivaled every kind of powerful destructive weather. Typhoons and tornadoes had nothing on him. She'd successfully avoided him for the past three weeks and she had been certain that fleeing her home country of Chantaine to visit her sisters in Texas would buy her even more time.

Who would have ever thought she would be caught staring at him at a charity social ball in Texas as he accepted an award for philanthropy? Phillipa knew that Nic had ties to Texas, but with his extensive business dealings, he had ties to many places.

The ballroom suddenly felt as if it was shrinking. Panic squeezed her chest. She had to get out. She had to catch her breath. Feeling her sister's curious gaze, she swallowed hard over the lump in her throat. "I'm not feeling well," she said. "Please excuse me."

When Bridget offered to come with her, Phillipa had to remain firm. "I'll be back in a little bit."

Sticking to the perimeter of the room as she fled, she kept her head down, hoping she wasn't drawing attention to herself. If she could just get out of this room, she would be fine, she told herself. Out of the room and away from Nic. Away from how he affected her.

She stepped out of the ballroom and held the door so it would catch softly as it closed, then took a few more steps away and leaned against the wall, which felt cool against her skin. Her sisters hadn't been exaggerating when they'd told her Texas summers were hell.

Phillipa took several deep breaths, willing her heart and mind to calm. How had she gotten herself into this? Why? Among her siblings, she'd done her best to maintain a low profile. As number five out of six strong personalities, it hadn't been that difficult. Her oldest brother, Stefan, had been born and bred to rule—everyone except his siblings anyway. Phillipa had found refuge in academia. It was much easier pleasing a few professors than being a princess and constantly making public appearances and dealing with the media. By nature, she'd always been an introvert. She'd never enjoyed crowded gatherings, hated posing for photographs and had little patience for all the effort it seemed to take to make her presentable.

When her first two sisters began to focus on their new husbands instead of royal duties, Phillipa had plunged herself into graduate studies to avoid being in the public eye. Her sister Bridget had seen through her plan and it had clearly irritated her, although Bridget had bucked up and done a fantastic job. The trouble now was that Bridget was determined to get a break and she had earned it. Phillipa cringed at the prospect of all the public appearances she would be forced to make.

"I'll be damned," a familiar male voice said, making her eyes pop open. "If it isn't the missing Her Highness Phillipa of Chantaine."

Phillipa stared into the dark gaze of Nic Lafitte and her lungs seemed to completely shut down. "I didn't know you would be here."

His mouth twisted in a half smile. "Why doesn't that surprise me?" he asked and slipped his hand around her arm. "Lucky for both of us that I am. We have unfinished business. You're coming with me. I can have my car delivered in seconds."

Her heart pounded. "I can't. My sisters expect me back for the rest of the event. They'll call the authorities if I go missing," she said.

"It wouldn't be the first time your family has tried

to get me in trouble with the law." He glanced around and tugged her down the hallway. "If you won't leave with me, then I'll take my moment somewhere else."

"Where are you taking me?" she asked. "This is crazy. I need to go back to my table. I need—" She broke off as he pushed open the door to a room marked Coat Closet and dragged her inside.

He pulled her to the back of the small room and gently, but firmly gripped her shoulders. "Tell me what you really need, Pippa. What do you really want?" he asked her in that dark, sexy voice that made her feel as if she were turning upside down.

A half-dozen images from the stolen moments they'd shared shot through her brain. The time they'd gone swimming at night. The afternoon she'd spent on his yacht. The walk they'd taken on the opposite side of the island when she'd learned so much about him and he'd made it so easy for her to talk about herself. Despite the bad blood between her family and his, Phillipa had never felt so drawn to another man in her life.

He lowered his head, holding her gaze until his mouth took hers. His kiss set off a riot of reaction and emotion inside her. He made her feel alive and out of control. She pulled back and whispered. "This is insane. It will never work. That's what I tried to tell you before."

"Why not?" he challenged her. Nic was always challenging her. Sometimes gently, sometimes with more strength. "If I want you and you want me, what is most important?"

Pippa bit her lip and struggled to remain rational. Members of her family had caused a lot of trouble by giving in to their emotions. She didn't want the same kind of trouble. "Want is a temporary emotion. There are more important things than temporary emotions."

"If that's true, why did you kiss me back? Why are you here with me right now?"

Pippa heard a gasp from the doorway and terror rushed through her. "Someone is here," she said. "We've got to get out of here," she said, stumbling toward the door. Nic helped to steady her as they stepped outside the closet.

Her sisters Bridget and Tina greeted them with furious disapproval stamped on their faces. Pippa inwardly cringed.

"Get away from my sister," Bridget said.

"That's for her to say, not you," Nic said.

"You're just using her," Tina said. "You only want her because she can redeem your terrible family name."

"Not everyone finds my family name reprehensible. Some even respect it," he said.

"That's respect you've bought with money," Tina said. "Leave Phillipa alone. You can never be good enough for her. If you have any compassion, you'll at least protect her reputation by leaving now."

Nic tightened his jaw. "I'll leave, but Phillipa will make the ultimate decision about the future of our relationship." He glanced behind him and met Phillipa's shocked, pale face. "*Ciao,* darling. Call me when you get some courage. Some things are meant to be," he said and strode away.

# Chapter One

*Seven Months Later*

She'd started running for exercise. That was what Pippa told her security detail anyway. She knew the truth. She was running from memories. Memories and the possibility that there was only one man for her and he was the one man she couldn't have.

"Stop it," she told herself, staring at the empty beach in front of her. Azure waves dappled onto white sands. By noon, there would be quite a few more bodies enjoying the beach. At six in the morning, however, she was the only one around. She debated turning on some music via her smartphone. She usually welcomed the noise, hoping it would drown out some of her thoughts. Today, she was searching for a little peace. Maybe the sound of the waves would help, she thought, and started out.

One foot in front of the other, she ran for two min-

utes, then walked for three. It was called interval train-
ing and the different paces suited her. Pippa had never
been athletic. From the time she'd learned to read, she'd
always been happiest with her nose stuck in a book.
Her nanny had been relieved because her brothers and
most of her sisters had been more demanding in one
way or another.

Running again, she inhaled the scent of the salt air.
The humidity was low today and she could feel the
moisture on her skin begin to evaporate. Slowing after
three minutes of running, she took a swig of her water
and trudged onward.

Along the shore, in the distance, she spotted a long
figure walking. She would wave and be friendly. Pippa
was a royal and Chantaine royals were not allowed to be
snooty. Other runners might be able to put their blinders
and zip past everyone in their path, but not a Devereaux.

As she drew closer, she saw that the figure was that
of a woman. Short white hair crowned her head, and a
sundress that resembled a nightgown covered her pe-
tite frame.

Pippa nodded. "Good morning," she said.

The woman looked away and stumbled.

Curious, Pippa vacillated as to whether to approach
her. Perhaps she was longing for solitude just as Pippa
was. The woman stumbled again and Pippa felt a twist
of concern. She walked toward the woman. "Pardon
me, may I help you?"

The woman shook her head. "No, no. I'm fine. It's so
beautiful here," she said in a lilting voice that contrasted
with the lines on her face and the frailness of her frame.

Something about her seemed familiar, but Pippa

couldn't quite identify it. The woman stumbled again, and Pippa's concern grew. Was she ill?

"Yes, the beach is lovely. Are you sure I can't help you? I could walk you back to where you started," she said. "Or perhaps you would like some water."

The woman's face crumpled. "No, no. Please don't make me go back. Please don't—" She broke off and collapsed right in front of Pippa.

Alarm shot through her. "Oh, my God!" she exclaimed and bent over the woman. This was *one* time when she would have loved to have had her security detail close by. Pippa put her arms around the woman and lifted her, surprised by her light weight. Glancing around, she pulled her toward a small stand of palm trees.

Frantic, she held the woman and gently shook her. "Please. Miss. Please." She spilled water from her bottle onto one of her hands and gently patted the woman's face. "Please wake up. Please."

Terrified that the woman was dying, she reached for her cell phone. The woman clearly needed emergency medical attention. Just as she put her finger over the speed dial for her security, the woman blinked her eyes. Huge and full of emotion, her eyes captivated Pippa.

She held her breath. "Are you all right? Please take a few sips of my water. It's clearly too hot out here for you. I'll call for help and—"

"No," the woman said with a strength that surprised Pippa. "Please don't do that." Then the woman closed her amazing, mesermizing eyes and began to sob.

The sound wrenched at Pippa. "You must let me help you."

"There's only one thing I want," she said and met Pippa's gaze again. "I just want to die in Chantaine."

Pippa gasped. Then a lightning flash of realization rocked through her. She looked at the woman and saw the resemblance of Nic in her eyes. His bone structure was a stronger, more masculine version, but his eyes were all Amelie. "Amelie," she whispered. "You're Amelie Lafitte."

The woman reluctantly nodded. "How do you know?"

"I know your son Nic." Pippa also knew that Amelie was in the final stages of cancer. Her time was drawing painfully close.

Amelie looked away. "I just wanted a little walk on the beach. I bet he's quite peeved that I left the yacht."

Peeved wasn't the word that came to Pippa's mind. "I'll call him for you," she said.

"Then all my fun will be over," she said with a cute pout. "He's such a worrywart."

Stunned at how quickly Amelie's spirit had returned, she hesitated a half beat, then dialed his cell. Despite the fact that she'd deleted it from her phone records months ago, every digit was engraved on her brain.

Five minutes later, a black Mercedes came to screeching halt on the curb of the road above the beach. Pippa immediately identified the dark figure exiting the driver's side of the vehicle. Nic. As he strode swiftly toward her and Amelie, she could see the tension in his frame. Seeing him after all these months set off a visceral response inside her. Her stomach clenched. Her heart beat unevenly.

"Hi, darling," Amelie said, remaining seated on the sand under the tree as she sipped Pippa's water. Pippa was still surprised at how quickly the woman had recovered after fainting. "Sorry to be a bother, but I woke up early and I just couldn't resist the chance to go for a walk on the beach."

"I would have been happy to walk with you," Nic said and turned to Pippa. What she wouldn't give to get a peek behind his dark sunglasses. "Thank you for calling me. I'll take her back to the yacht now and you can continue your run. I didn't know you were a runner."

She felt her face heat with self-consciousness. "I'm more of a combination walker and runner."

He nodded and glanced back at his mother. "Dad's beside himself with worry. It was all I could do to keep him from tearing after you."

"Paul can't hobble with crutches let alone tear after me with that broken foot of his. The doctor said it will be ten more weeks before he can put any weight on it at all," she said, then turned her head thoughtfully to the side. "You know what I'm in the mood for? Crepes. There used to be a wonderful café on the edge of town. They made the most delicious crepes."

"Bebe's on Oleander," Pippa said. "It's still there, and Bebe's granddaughter helps makes the crepes."

"Oh," Amelie said, clasping her hands together. "It's still there. We must go. And we can bring one back for Paul." She turned to Pippa. "You must come, too."

Pippa blinked at the invitation and slid a quick helpless glance at Nic.

"Mother, do you know who Pippa is?" he asked as he extended his hand to help her rise to her feet.

Amelie studied her for a long moment and frowned. "She looks a bit familiar. I can't quite." Her eyes widened. "Oh, dear. You're a Devereaux. I can see it in your eyes and your chin. Oh, dear. This could get a bit messy."

"Just a little," Nic said in a wry tone. "But let's give her the choice. Would you like to join us for crepes, Your Highness?"

Pippa heard the hint of goading challenge in Nic's voice. She'd heard it before, but it seemed to hold more of an edge than ever. The truth was she didn't want her photo taken with Nic and his mother. To say it could cause problems was a huge understatement.

"That's okay," he said before she could respond. "Thanks again for looking out for my mother. Ci—"

"I'm coming," Pippa said impulsively. "Unless you're rescinding the invitation," she tossed back at him in her own challenging voice.

He paused a half beat and tilted his head as if she'd taken him off guard. The possibility thrilled her. "Not at all. Would you like to ride with us in my vehicle?"

"Thank you, but no. I'll drive myself and meet you in about fifteen minutes," Pippa said and turned her gaze to Amelie. "I'll see you soon. Please drink some more fluids."

"Thank you, darling. Isn't she delightful?" she said to Nic. "She fusses just like you do."

"Yes," he said in a dry tone. "Delightful."

Fifteen minutes later as Pippa put a ball cap on her head and adjusted her large pair of sunglasses, she wondered if she'd lost her mind agreeing to join Nic and his mother, the notorious Amelie, for crepes. Glancing in the rearview mirror, she could easily imagine the horror on the face of the royal advisers. Running on the beach at 6:00 a.m. in her current state was one thing, but walking into a public place of business was quite another. She thought of Nic's goading attitude and made a face at the mirror. Well, she couldn't back down now. Stepping from her car, she could only hope she wouldn't be recognized.

Because she'd spent far less time in the public eye than her siblings, that was on her side. Her hair, however, was very distinctive and not in a good way. Wavy and brown with a tendency to frizz, she hoped she'd concealed it adequately by pulling it back in a ponytail and covering it with a cap.

She walked into the old but elegant eating establishment that featured every kind of crepe one could imagine. As soon as she stepped inside, she spotted Amelie, who also saw her and lifted her hand in a wave. Nic, sitting opposite Amelia, turned his head around to look at her and also waved. His gaze said he was surprised she'd shown up, which irritated Pippa.

She walked to the booth where Amelia and Nic sat and sank onto the red vinyl seat.

"Lovely that you joined us," Amelie said and smiled as she lifted a menu. "How shall I choose? I want one of everything."

Enchanted, Pippa picked up the menu. The array of choices was vast and mind-boggling. "What are you in the mood for?"

"Something sweet," Amelie said. "Sweet, fruity. Oh, no, chocolate, too." She shrugged helplessly.

The waitress approached. "*Bonjour*. How can I help you? Coffee?"

"Yes," Amelie said. "Café au lait."

"Tea," Pippa said.

"Coffee, black," Nic said. "Ladies, any idea what you want to order?"

"Apricot crepes. Strawberries and cream. Chocolate hazelnut. Banana cream." Amelie paused.

Wondering how the woman could possibly consume that many crepes, she exchanged a quick glance with Nic, who shook his head and rubbed his jaw. She glanced back at Amelie. "Do you want anything with protein?"

"Not particularly," Nic's mother said.

"And you?" Pippa asked Nic.

He shrugged. "I'm here for the ride."

"Can you please also bring us the crepe suzette and some carryout boxes?" Pippa asked the server.

"No problem, ma'am," she said and stared at Pippa for a long moment. "Pardon me, you look familiar."

Pippa fought a sliver of panic and held her breath. *Please don't recognize me.*

"Are you a newscaster?"

Relief rushed through her, making her almost giddy. She shook her head and smiled. "Nope, I'm just a university student. Thanks for the compliment, though."

The server's face was sheepish. "No trouble. I'll have your order up as soon as possible."

"Thank you so very much," Pippa said and after the server left, she felt the gazes of both Nic and Amelie.

Amelie sighed, lifting her shoulders and smiling with a charm that lit up the room and Pippa suddenly realized who the woman resembled. Gamin with super-expressive eyes, Amelie could have been a white-haired twin of Audrey Hepburn. "It's so wonderful to be here again. Magic. The smell is divine. I should have come back sooner, so I'll just make up for it today."

"You don't want to make yourself sick," Nic said.

"Of course not. I'll just take a bite of each, and we can take the rest back to Paul." Amelie's smile fell and she made a tsking sound. "Poor Paul. He's in such pain with his foot."

She said it as if she suffered no pain herself, but Pippa knew she did. She took a quick glance at Nic and caught the tightening of his jaw. She was struck by Amelie's determination to grab at every experience in life and Nic's struggle to hide a myriad of the emotions he was experiencing.

"I've heard the recovery from a broken foot can be a bear," Pippa said.

"Oh, and trust me, Paul is a being a complete bear," Amelie said. "He doesn't like being restrained. Never has." Amelie glanced at Nic. "It runs in the family." She turned back to Pippa with an expressive, interested gaze. "But enough about us. Tell me about you, your interests, your life. Over the years, I've read a few stories in the news about the Devereauxs, and I must confess I wondered about Edward's children. I'm sure he must have been proud of all of you."

Pippa paused. The truth was her father hadn't been very involved with any of his children. He'd given the most attention to her brother Stefan because he would be the heir, but her father was mostly pleased that he had enough children to do the work, so he could spend more time playing on his yacht. Often with women other than his wife.

"I've always been a bit of a bookworm. I'm working on my doctorate in genealogy with a specialization on the medical impact on the citizens of Chantaine. My brother Stefan is determined to improve the health care of our people, so he has approved my path of studies."

"That's fascinating," Amelie said. "What have you learned so far?"

"Like many countries, our people are more susceptible to some diseases and conditions than others. These can be traced back hundreds of years to the introduction of different immigrants, new foods and changes in our environment. The neurological disease that struck down my father can be traced back to his great-great-grandmother's family. There are also certain cancers that became more common such as when Chantaine experienced a large immigration from Iceland."

Amelie gave a slow nod. "I wonder if—" She glanced up and broke off with a smile. "The crepes are here."

Just as she'd said, Amelie only took a bite of each crepe. She savored each bite, closing her eyes and making a *mmm* sound. "I'm tempted to eat more, but I know it would be a mistake." She leaned toward Pippa and extended her hand. "Dear, I must tell you that even though I couldn't marry your father all those years ago, I wished him only the very best after we parted. I hope he was happy."

Pippa tried to think of how to respond to Amelie's words. The story about Edward and Amelie's courtship was the stuff of tabloids. Before he'd taken the throne, Prince Edward had fallen for Amelie and Amelie had been entranced by him for a short while. When she'd met Paul Lafitte, from the States, however, she'd fallen for the tall, dark Texan hook, line and sinker. The Lafittes descended from pirates and even Pippa had to agree the Lafitte men held a dark, irresistible charm.

When Amelie tried to break off her engagement, Prince Edward had refused. Paul had intervened on her behalf and there'd been a terrible brawl. Her father the prince had been humiliated and Pippa wasn't certain he'd ever truly given his heart away again.

"I think he enjoyed his life," Pippa finally said. "He loved his yacht and the sea and we always felt glad that he was able to indulge his passion."

Amelie patted Pippa's hand. "You're a lovely girl. As they say in Texas, you do him proud. Now, if you'll both excuse me while I powder my nose," she said and stood.

Nic also stood. "Need an escort?" he asked.

"Not this time, darling. Maybe you can talk Pippa into nibbling on some of those crepes," she said and walked away.

"Is she okay?" Pippa asked when he sat down.

He shrugged. "For the moment. The next moment could bring something totally different. She knows her time is short and she's decided to make the most of it. The only problem is she's turned into an eight-year-old. Impulsive, runs off without thinking. With my father down due to his broken foot, I've become her keeper."

Pippa swallowed over the knot of emotion in her throat and began to put the crepes in the carryout boxes. "I'm sure it's difficult. On the one hand, you want to give her everything she wants. On the other, you want to keep her safe. It's an impossible situation. She told me," she said, biting her lip, "that she wants to die in Chantaine."

His gaze narrowed. "That's going to be a tough wish to fulfill given the fact that my father isn't allowed to set foot on Chantaine."

Cold realization rushed through her. "I forgot all about that. I can't believe that would be enforced after all these years."

He gave a rough chuckle. "After all these years, your family still hates me. I can't take the chance that your family would lock him up in prison."

"It wouldn't be my family. It's a silly law," she said.

"Same result. It sucks, but Amelie can't have every wish on her bucket list. I'll do my damn best to make sure she gets as many as I can," he said and stood as his mother arrived at the table.

Amelie met his gaze and sighed. "We should leave, shouldn't we?"

He nodded and placed the boxes in a bag.

"Let me look around just one more moment," she said, surveying the room as if she wanted to savor each detail, the same way she'd savored each bite of the crepes. "I've already spoken to Bebe. She's lovely as is her granddaughter. *Ciao*," she whispered and picked up the bag, then led the way to the door.

A terrible helplessness tore at Pippa as she followed Amelie out the door. She felt Nic's presence behind her and tried to tamp down the painful knot in her chest. Seeing him again had been like ripping off a bandage before the wound was healed. She'd thought the longing she'd felt for him before was awful, but now it was even worse. Knowing that he was facing some of his darkest days and that she shouldn't, couldn't, help him, was untenable. Meeting his magical mother face-to-face and seeing her courage and joy made her feel like a wimp. Her biggest challenge to date was writing her dissertation.

Amelie stopped beside Nic's Mercedes and turned to Pippa. "I hope we meet again, Your Highness. You're the nicest princess I've ever met. I'm sorry I frightened you with my annoying fainting spell. But then you gave me water and helped me remember Bebe's. I certainly came out the winner in this situation."

"I beg to differ," Pippa said. "It was my great pleasure to meet you."

"*Ciao,* darling princess," she said and Nic opened the door for her.

Pippa should have turned away, but she couldn't resist one more look at his face. It was the worst kind of craving imaginable.

He turned and met her gaze for a heart-stopping moment that took her breath away. "*Ciao,* Princess."

Still distracted by her encounter with Nic and his mother after she'd returned to the palace, Pippa started down the hallway to her living quarters. She would need to set the Lafittes' situation aside if she was going to make any progress on her research today, and heaven knows, progress had been very slow coming since she'd made the insane mistake of getting involved with Nic. The problem was that even after she'd broken off with him, he still haunted her so much that she struggled to get her work done.

Just as she turned the corner toward her quarters,

she heard a shrill scream from the other wing. *Tyler,* she thought, easily identifying one her sister's toddler stepsons. He was going through a screaming stage.

"Tyler, darling, you're not dressed," her sister Bridget called, her voice echoing down the marble hallways. "Don't—"

Pippa heard Tyler cackle with glee. She also heard the sound of her sister's heels as she ran after him. Chuckling to herself, she wondered when Bridget would learn that toddlers and high heels didn't go together. She rushed down the hall and turned another corner, spotting Tyler running toward her in all his naked glory. Bridget followed with Travis in her arms.

"Oh, Pippa, you saved my life. Can you grab him? The little beast thinks it's funny to run all over the palace bloody naked."

Tyler shrieked when he saw Pippa and skidded to a stop. Glancing over his shoulder at Bridget bearing down on him, he knew he was caught. Pippa scooped him up in her arms before he had a chance to get away.

"What are you doing? Did you just get a bath?" Pippa asked and buried her nose in his shoulder, making him laugh. "You smell like a deliciously clean little boy."

"Thank you so much," Bridget said breathlessly. "At least I got a diaper on Travis."

As soon as she stepped within touching distance, Tyler flung himself at her. "Mumma," he said and pressed an open mouth kiss against Bridget's cheek.

Bridget squeezed him against her and shifted Travis on her hip. "Now, you get all lovey-dovey," she said and gave him a kiss in return.

"Where are the nannies?" Pippa asked and held out

her hands to Travis. He fell into her arms, then stuck his thumb in his mouth.

"I gave Claire the morning off and Maria had to take care of an emergency with her mother," she said. "I had planned to check on the ranch Ryder and I are having built." Bridget rolled her eyes and laughed. "I never dreamed Stefan would permit a ranch to be built on Chantaine."

"I never would have dreamed you would live on a ranch with twin stepchildren."

"They're not steppies to me," Bridget said. "Ryder and I are in the process of making it all legal. The little perfect, gorgeous beasties will be mine just as much as they are his."

"Would you like me to watch the boys while you go check on the new house?" Pippa offered. Because Chantaine was an island, new construction was a long process and she knew both Bridget and Ryder were eager for their own place.

"I feel like I take advantage of you far too often. I know I'm not helping you get caught up on your studies...."

Pippa felt a sinking sensation in her stomach. Bridget and the boys weren't the real reason she'd had a difficult time focusing on her studies. "It's not as if you'll be gone all day," she said.

"True," Bridget said. "Only an hour or two. You're the perfect sister," Bridget said, leaning forward to give Pippa a kiss on the cheek. "Let's go back to my quarters so I can at least get my little nudist dressed before I leave."

Pippa smiled as she followed Bridget down the hall

and into her family's suite of rooms. "I think it's your outlook that has changed. Since you got married to Ryder, everything's close to perfection."

"That just goes to show the power of having a good man in your life," Bridget said. "As soon as I have more than half a moment, I must get to work on finding one for you."

Alarm shot through Pippa. "Oh, so not necessary. I still have to finish my work for my PhD."

"That won't be forever," Bridget said as she dressed wiggly Tyler.

"I can only hope," Pippa muttered.

"It won't be," Bridget said emphatically. "Besides, you can't wait forever to move on, romantically speaking. I can help with that."

"You seem to forget that our family is dreadful when it comes to matchmaking," Pippa said. "How much did you enjoy Stefan's attempts at matchmaking?"

Bridget waved her hand in a dismissive gesture. "That's different. I won't be trying to match you up with someone who can contribute to Chantaine. I'll find someone hot and entertaining."

"Lovely intentions," Pippa said. "Don't strain yourself. The boys and I will have some fun in the playroom."

"Perfect. If I'm late they can have lunch in an hour."

"Will do," Pippa said. "Are you truly going to have cattle at this ranch?"

"If Ryder has his way," Bridget said with a sigh. "If we have to take the man out of Texas, we'll just bring Texas to him. *Ciao.* I'll be back soon," she said and kissed both of the boys.

As soon as Bridget left, the twin toddlers looked at her with pouty faces. Travis's lower lip protruded and he began to whimper. Tyler joined in.

"Absolutely none of that. She'll be back before you know it." Bridget set both of them on their feet and took them by the hand. "To the playroom," she said and marched them into the small backroom. If there was one thing she'd learned about caring for toddlers, it was that it helped to be willing to make a bloody fool of herself. She immediately turned on the animal sounds CD and followed the instructions to make honking sounds. The boys dried up and joined her.

Just over an hour later, Bridget returned and Pippa could no longer escape her studies. She retreated to her room with a half sandwich for lunch. She thought of the crepes and her stomach clenched. Her mind kept wandering to the time she'd spent with Nic and his mother.

She told herself not to think about it. It wasn't her responsibility. These genealogy charts required her complete and immediate attention. She'd used every possible device to procrastinate doing her work entirely too long. Inputting her second cousin's name to the chart, she forced herself to focus. Whenever she conducted her research on people whom she knew, she often thought about their personal stories. Her second cousin Harold had moved to Tibet and his sister, Georgina, had married a man from England and was raising her children in the countryside. Pippa had always liked Georgina because she'd been such a down-to-earth sort of woman. It was a shame she didn't see her more often.

Harold and Georgina's deceased parents had owned a lovely cottage on the other side of Chantaine that was now left vacant because neither Harold nor Georgina visited Chantaine very often. Why, in fact, Pippa was certain it had been nearly eight years since either of her second cousins had set foot on Chantaine.

Pippa stopped dead, staring at the cursor on her laptop. *Vacant lovely cottage. Nic's parents.*

"Stop it," she hissed to herself. It would be incredibly disloyal. If her brother Stefan ever found out, he would never forgive her. And there was no way he wouldn't find out. Not with her security haunting her. She was lucky she'd escaped discovery today.

*Back to work,* she told herself sternly and worked past midnight. She finally crawled into bed, hopeful she would fall into deep sleep. Thank goodness, she did. Sometime during the night, she sank into a dream where a black limo crawled through a beautiful cemetery. Cars and people dressed in black but carrying flowers followed the limo. Everything inside her clinched with pain. A white butterfly fluttered over the black limo, capturing her attention. It could have been the spirit of...

Pippa suddenly awakened, disoriented, the images of the limo and the butterfly mingling in her mind. She sat up in bed, her heart slamming into her chest. Images of her brother Stefan, Nic, his mother, Amelie.

This wasn't her business, she told herself. Her heart ached for Nic and his mother, but she couldn't go against her family to make his mother's dream come true. She just couldn't. It wouldn't be right. It would be a terrible betrayal.

She tried to catch her breath and closed her eyes.

She tried to make her brain stop spinning. How could she possibly deceive her family for Nic? For Amelie?

But how could she not?

## Chapter Two

It took most of the rest of the day to catch up with her cousin to get permission to use the cottage. Georgina was so gracious that it made Pippa feel guilty. Oh, well, if she was going to go through with providing the cottage for Nic's mother and father, then her web of deception was just getting started. The choice to deceive her family was unforgivable, but the choice to turn her back on Amelie was more unacceptable. Her stomach churned because she wasn't a dishonest person. The prospect of all the lies she would have to tell put a bad taste in her mouth.

She would normally try to reason with Stefan, but Pippa knew her entire family was unreasonable about the Lafitte matter. She would have to learn to push aside her slimy feelings about this and press on. The first task was to call Nic.

* * *

Nic studied the recent reports from his and his father's business on his tablet PC while he drank a glass of Scotch. He took a deep breath of the Mediterranean night air as he sat on the deck of his yacht anchored close enough to shore for his mother to catch a glimpse of her precious Chantaine whenever she liked. He just hoped she didn't do anything impulsive like jump overboard and swim to shore. Rubbing his chin, he shuddered at what a nightmare that would be. He couldn't put it past her, though, especially after she'd sneaked off the other morning.

Nic was caught somewhere between genie and parent, and he wasn't equipped to be either. The reports on both his father's businesses and his own looked okay for the moment, but he knew he would have to go back to the States soon for his father's company. With Amelie's illness, Paul Lafitte had understandably been distracted. Despite the fact that they'd separated on two different occasions, Amelie was the light of Paul's life and Nic wasn't sure how his father would survive after his mother... Nic didn't even want to think the word, let alone say it, even though he knew the time was coming.

Sighing, he took another sip of his Scotch and heard the vibrating buzz of his cell phone. The number on the caller ID surprised him. After his surprise meeting with Princess Pippa the other morning, he figured he'd never see her again except for public affairs.

He picked up the phone and punched the call button. "Nic Lafitte. Your Highness, what a surprise," he said, unable to keep the bite from his voice. Pippa had turned out to be the tease of his life.

"Hello. I hope I'm not interrupting anything," she said, her voice tense with nerves, which made him curious.

"Just a perfect glass of Scotch and rare solitude," he said.

A short silence followed. "Well, pardon the interruption, but I have some news that may be of interest to you."

"You called to tell me you missed me," he said, unable to resist the urge to bother her. During and after their little interlude last year, the woman had bothered the hell out of him.

He heard her sharp intake of breath and realized he'd scored. "I called about your mother."

His pleasure immediately diminished. "What about her? Have you discussed the situation with your family, and now they won't even allow her and my father in the harbor?"

"No, of course not," Pippa said. "If you would just let me finish—"

"Go ahead," he said, the semi-peacefulness of the evening now ruined.

"I found a cottage for your parents where they can stay," she said.

Nic blinked in sudden, silent surprise.

"Nic, did you hear me?"

"Yes. Repeat that please."

"I found a cottage for your parents on Chantaine," she said.

"Why?" he demanded.

Another gap of silence followed. "Um, well, I have these cousins Georgina and Harry and neither of them live in Chantaine anymore. They haven't even visited in years, and they inherited a cottage from their parents. It's been vacant, again for years, so I thought, why not?"

"Exactly," Nic said. "Why not? Except for the fact that my father has been banned from setting foot on Chantaine. I don't suppose your brother experienced a sudden wave of compassion, or just a rational moment and has decided to pardon Paul Lafitte."

"You don't need to insult Stefan," she said. "My brother is just defending my father's honor."

"Even though Stefan wouldn't have been born if your father had married Amelie," Nic said.

"Yes, I know it's not particularly logical, but the point is I have found this house. Your mother wants more time in Chantaine. Staying there can make it happen."

"You still haven't addressed the issue about my father," Nic said.

"Well, I thought we could work around that. Your mother mentioned that he broke his foot, so it's not as if he'll be able to tour much. When he does, perhaps he could wear a hat and glasses."

"And a fake mustache?" he added, rolling his eyes. It was a ludicrous plan.

"I know it's not perfect," she said.

"Far from it," he said.

"But it's better than nothing."

"I can't take the chance that my father will end up in jail."

"Perhaps that's not your decision to make," she countered, surprising him.

"What do you mean by that?"

"I mean shouldn't he be given the choice?" she asked. "Besides, your father's presence may never be discovered. It's not as if there are copies of his photo posted everywhere the way you do in the States."

"It's called a Wanted Poster, and they're mostly just displayed in post offices and convenience stores these days. We've progressed since the Wild West days," he said.

"Exactly," she said. "And so have we. No one has been beheaded in over one hundred and fifty years, and we haven't used the dungeon as a prison for nearly a hundred."

"Why don't I feel better? I know that Chantaine doesn't operate under the policy of innocent until proven guilty. Your judicial system, and I use the term loosely, moves slower than the process of turning coal into diamonds."

"I didn't call to debate my country's judicial system. I called to offer a place to stay for your mother and father. If you want it, I shall arrange to have it cleaned and prepared for them. Otherwise…" She paused and he heard her take a breath.

"Otherwise?" he prompted.

"Otherwise, *ciao,*" she said and hung up on him.

Nic blinked again. Princess Pippa wasn't the rollover he'd thought she was. He downed the rest of his exquisite Scotch, barely tasting it. What the hell. She had surprised him. Now he had to make a decision. Although his father had caused trouble for the entire family, Nic felt protective of him, especially in his father's current state with his broken foot and his grief over Amelie.

Nic closed his eyes and swore under his breath. He

already knew how his father would respond if given the choice of risking prosecution in Chantaine. Paul Lafitte was a blustering bear and bull. He would love the challenge...even if he was in traction and confined to the house.

Raking his hand through his hair, he knew what he had to do. He walked inside to the stateroom lounge where his father dozed in front of the television. A baseball game was playing and his father was propped in an easy chair snoring.

Maybe he should wait until tomorrow, Nic thought and turned off the television.

His father gave a loud snort and his eyes snapped open. "What happened? Who's ahead?"

"Rangers," Nic lied. The Rangers were having a terrible season.

"Yeah, and I'm the Easter bunny," his father said.

Nic gave a dry laugh. His father was selective with the use of denial, and apparently he wasn't going to exercise that muscle with the Rangers tonight. "Good luck hopping," he said. "You need anything to drink?"

"Nah. Take a seat. What's on your mind? I can tell something's going on," he said, waving his hand as if the yacht belonged to him instead of Nic.

Nic sank onto the sofa next to his father. "I got an interesting call tonight."

"Must have been a woman. Was she pregnant?" his father asked.

Nic gave a short laugh. "Nothing like that. I've been offered a cottage where you and Mom can stay. On Chantaine."

His dad gave a low whistle. "How did you manage that?"

Nic shrugged. "Lucky, I guess. The problem is you still have legal issues in Chantaine."

His dad smiled and rubbed his mouth. "So I do, and punching Prince Edward in the face after he insulted your mother was worth it ten times over."

"Easy to say, but if you stay in Chantaine, there's a possibility that you could get caught." Nic shook his head. "Dad, with their legal system, you could be stuck in jail for a while."

"So?" he asked.

"So, it's a risk. You're not the young buck you once were. You could end up stuck there while Mom is…" He didn't want to say the rest.

His father narrowed his eyes. It was an expression Nic had seen several times on his father's face. The dare a pirate couldn't deny. He descended from wily pirates. His father was no different, although his father had gotten caught a few times. "Your mother wants to rest in Chantaine. We'll accept the kind offer of your friend. To hell with the Devereauxs."

"Might not want to go that far," Nic said, thinking another glass of Scotch was in order. "A Devereaux is giving you the cottage."

"Well, now that sounds like quite the story," his father said, his shaggy eyebrows lifted high on his forehead.

"Another time," Nic said. "You need to rest up for your next voyage."

His father gave a mysterious smile. "If my great-

great-grandfather escaped the authorities on a peg leg, I can do it with a cast."

Nic groaned. "No need to push it, Dad."

The next morning, he dialed the princess.

"Hello," she said in a sleep-sexy voice that did weird things to his gut.

"This is Nic. We'll accept your kind offer. Meet me at the cottage and I'll clean it. The less people involved, the better."

Silence followed. "I didn't think of that," she confessed. "I'm accustomed to staff taking oaths of silence."

He smiled at her naïveté. "This is a different game. Too many people need to be protected. You, my mother and father. We need to keep this as quiet and low-profile as possible."

"Okay. I'll meet you at the cottage mid-morning," she said.

"What about your security?" he asked.

"I'll tell them I'm going to the library," she said.

"Won't they follow you?"

"I'll go to the library first. They'll get bored. They always do."

"Who are these idiots on your security detail?" he asked.

"Are you complaining?"

"No," he said. "And yes."

She laughed, and the breathless sound made his chest expand. He suddenly felt lighter. "How do you end up with the light end of the security detail?"

"I'm boring. I don't go clubbing. I've never been on

drugs. I babysit my nieces and nephews. I study genealogy, for bloody's sake."

He nodded, approving her M.O. "Well done, but does that fence ever feel a little too tall for you? Ever want to climb out?"

"I climb out when I want," she said in a cool voice. "I'll see you this afternoon around 1:00 p.m. The address is 307 Sea Breeze. *Ciao,*" she said and hung up before he could reply.

Nic pulled the phone away from his ear and stared at it. He was unaccustomed to having anyone hang up on him, let alone a woman. He must have really gotten under Pippa's skin to affect her manners that way. The possibility brought him pleasure. Again, he liked the idea of *bothering* her.

Just before one, he pulled past the overgrown hedges of the driveway leading to an expansive bungalow. Looked like there was a separate guest bedroom. Dibs, he thought. He could sleep there and keep track of his parents while keeping on top of the businesses.

He stopped his car behind another—Pippa's. He recognized it from the other day. Curious, he stepped from his vehicle and walked to the front door and knocked. He waited. No answer. He knocked again.

No answer again, so he looked at the doorknob and picked the lock. Pirates had their skills. He opened the door and was shocked speechless at the sight in front of him. Pippa, dressed in shorts and a T-shirt with her wild hair pulled back in a ponytail, was vacuuming the den.

The princess had a very nice backside, which he enjoyed watching for a full moment...okay, two.

Pippa turned and spotted him, screaming and dropping the vacuum handle. She clutched her throat with her hands. The appliance made a loud groan of protest.

"Did you consider knocking?" she demanded.

He lifted two fingers, then pulled up the vacuum cleaner handle and turned it off. "Twice. You didn't answer. I would have never dreamed you could be a cleaning fairy. This is a stretch."

"I spent a couple summers in a rustic camp in Norway. Cleaning was compulsory. We also cleaned the homes of several of the camp leaders."

"You didn't mention this to your parents?" he asked.

She laughed. "I didn't speak to my parents very often. I mentioned something about it to my nanny after the second summer and was never sent back after that. The cleaning wasn't that bad. The camp had a fabulous library and no one edited my reading choices. Heaven for me," she said.

"Will clean for books?" he said.

She smiled and met his gaze. "Something like that."

He held her gaze for a long moment and saw the second that her awareness of him hit her. Breaking the visual connection, she cleared her throat. "Well, I should get back to work."

"Anything special you want me to do?"

"Mop the floors if you don't mind. I've already dusted the entire house, but haven't touched the guest quarters outside. I think it would also be a good idea for you to assess the arrangement of the furniture throughout the house for any special needs your parents may have, such as your father's foot problem. We don't want him tripping and prolonging his recovery."

"I don't know. It might be a good thing if my father is immobile. He could cause trouble when he's full strength," Nic said. "He's always been a rebellious, impulsive man. I hate to say it, but he might just take a trip out of the house so he can feel like he's flying in the face of your family."

Pippa winced. "He wouldn't admit his name, would he?"

"I hope not. That's part of the reason I wasn't sure this was a good idea," he said.

"What made you change your mind?"

"You did. My father will be okay if he's reminded that his responsibility is to make this time for my mother as trouble-free as possible. I'll make sure he gets that message in multiple modalities every day."

"Thank you very much," she said.

"If you're so terrified that your family will find out, why did you take this risk for yourself? Your relationship with your brothers and sisters will never be the same if they know you did this."

She took a deep breath and closed her eyes for a half beat as if to bolster her determination. "I hate the idea of disappointing my brothers and sisters. I hate it more than you can imagine, but I wouldn't be able to live with myself if I could help your mother with this one wish if I had the ability. And I have the ability."

"I'll do what I can to make sure the rest of the Devereauxs don't find out. I haven't told my mother yet about the cottage. She's going to be very excited."

Pippa smiled. "I hope so."

"Thanks," he said. "I'll go check out the bedrooms."

An hour later, after Pippa finished vacuuming and tackled the kitchen, she found Nic cleaning the hall bathroom. It was an ironic sight. Hot six-foot-four international businessman scrubbing the tub. Just as he wouldn't expect to find her turn into a cleaning machine, she wouldn't expect the same of him, either. She couldn't help admiring the way his broad shoulders followed the shape of a V to his waist. Even in a T-shirt, the man looked great from behind. Bloody shame for her. *Get your mind out of the gutter.*

He turned around before she had a chance to clear her throat or utter a syllable. She stared at him speechless for a second, fearing he could read her mind. *Not possible,* she told herself as she felt her cheeks heat with embarrassment.

"Can I help you?" he asked.

In too many ways, she thought, but refused to dwell on them. "I'm almost finished with the kitchen, and it occurred to me that it might be a good idea to arrange for some groceries to be picked up for your parents before they arrive."

"Groceries?" he echoed.

"Yes, I was hoping you could help with a list."

He made a face. "I don't do a lot of grocery shopping. My housekeeper takes care of that."

"I have less experience with grocery shopping that I do with cleaning. That's why I thought we could send someone."

"Who can we trust?" he asked.

She winced. "Excellent point."

"After we move them in, I'll just arrange for a member of my staff from the yacht to take care of house and shopping duties," he said. "But unless we want to delay their move-in, it looks like we'll need to do the initial run ourselves."

"We?" she squeaked.

"I didn't think it would be nice to ask you to do it by yourself," he said.

But it had clearly crossed his mind. She frowned.

"Will that put you a little close for comfort to the plebeians?"

"No," she told him, detesting the superior challenging expression on his face. "I was just trying to remember if I'd left my cap in my vehicle."

"I have an extra," he said. "I'll take you in my car."

"What about the list?"

"We'll wing it," he said.

Moments later, she grabbed her cap from her car and perched her oversize sunglasses on her nose. She didn't bother to look at her reflection. After spending the afternoon cleaning, she knew she didn't look like anyone's idea of a princess. Nic opened the passenger door for her and she slid into his car.

After he climbed into the driver's side, the space inside his Mercedes seemed to shrink. She inhaled to compensate for the way her lungs seemed to narrow at Nic's proximity, but only succeeded in drawing in a draft of the combination of his masculine scent and subtle but sexy cologne. He pulled out of the driveway.

"Which way to the nearest market?" he asked.

Pippa blinked. She had no idea.

"Here," he said, handing her his phone. "Find one on my smartphone."

It took a couple moments, and Nic had to backtrack, but they were moving in the right direction.

"I'm thinking eggs, milk, bread and perhaps some fruit," she said, associating each item with one of her fingers. It was a memory trick she'd taught herself when she was young. The only problem was when she ran out of fingers.

"Chocolate, cookies and wine," Nic added. "A bakery cake if we can find it. My mother's priority for eating healthy went down the tubes after her last appointment with the doctor. My dad will want booze and carbs. His idea of health food is a pork roast with a loaded baked potato."

"Oh, my," she said, trying to wrap her head around Nic's list versus hers. "I hope we can find—"

"They'll be happy with whatever we get for the first twenty-four hours," Nic said as he pulled into the parking lot. "Let's just do this fast," he added and pulled on a ball cap of his own. "The faster we move, the less chance you have of being discovered."

"I think I'm well-disguised," she said as he opened the door and helped her out of the car.

"Until you open your mouth," he said.

"What do you mean by that?"

He led her toward the door of the market. "I mean you have a refined, distinctive voice, PD. A combination of husky sweet and so proper you could have been in Regency England."

"PD," she echoed, then realized PD stood for Pippa Devereaux. "Well, at least I *look* ordinary," she huffed.

He stopped beside her. "And I don't," he said, tugging on his ball cap.

She allowed herself a forbidden moment of looking at him from head to toe. He could have been dressed in rags and he would be sexy. She swallowed an oath. "You don't know the meaning of ordinary," she said and walked in front of him.

Hearing Nic grab a cart behind her, she moved toward the produce. "Surely, they'd enjoy some fruit. Your mother seemed to favor fruit crepes the other day."

"They were wrapped in sugar," he said as she picked up a bunch of bananas and studied them. "In the basket," he instructed. "We have a need for speed, PD."

"I'm not sure I like being called PD," she said, fighting a scowl as she put the bananas in the cart.

He pressed his mouth against her ear. "Would you prefer PP instead? For Princess Pippa?"

A shiver of awareness raced through her and she quickly stepped away. "Not at all," she said and picked up an apricot. "Does this look ripe?"

"It's perfect," he said, swiping it from her hand and added two more to the cart. "Now, move along."

She shot him an affronted look but began to walk. "No one except my brothers or sisters would dream of speaking to me that way."

"One of my many charms, PD," he said and tossed a loaf of bread into the cart.

Moments later, after throwing several items into the cart, they arrived at the register. Pippa picked up a bag of marshmallows.

"Good job," he said.

"I thought they could make that camping dessert you Americans eat," Pippa said. She'd read about it in a book.

"Camping treat?" he echoed.

"Some More of something," she said.

His eyes widened. "S'mores," he said. "We need chocolate bars and graham crackers. Get him to hold you," he said and strode away.

*"Hold me?"* she said at the unfamiliar expression and caught the cashier studying her. He was several years younger than she was with rings and piercing in places that made her think *ouch*.

He leaned toward her. "If you need holding, I can help you after I finish my shift," he said in a low voice.

Embarrassment flooded through her. She was rarely in a position for a man to flirt with her. Her brother usually set her up with men at least twenty years older, who wouldn't dare make an improper advance, so she wasn't experienced with giving a proper response. "The grocery order," she finally managed. "I was repeating what my, uh, friend said. He misspoke, as he often does. The grocery order need holding."

The cashier looked disappointed. "The customer behind you is ready."

Pippa considered pulling royal rank, but knew it would only hurt her in the end, so she stepped aside and allowed the person behind her with a mammoth order go first.

Less than a moment later, Nic appeared with chocolate bars and graham crackers. He glanced at the person in front of her and frowned. "How did that happen? I told you to hold the cashier."

"There was a mix-up and he thought I wanted, uh, him for reasons other than his professional duties. When I refused his kind invitation, he felt spurned and allowed the customer behind me to proceed." She sighed. "Do all men have such delicate egos?"

Nic lifted a dark brow before he pulled his sunglasses over his eyes. "Depends on how many mixed messages we get. Poor guy."

## Chapter Three

"Are you sure you want to read to Stephenia tonight?" Eve Jackson Devereaux, the wife to the crown prince of Chantaine, asked in her Texas twang as she walked with Pippa to her stepdaughter's room inside the royal master suite. "You look a little tired."

"I wouldn't dream of missing it. You and Stefan enjoy a few extra moments this evening. You deserve it."

"You are a dream sister," Eve said.

Pippa felt her heart squeeze at how Eve left off at the in-law. "As are you," she said and studied her sister-in-law. "You look like you could use a long night's rest yourself."

Eve frowned and pressed her hands to her cheeks. "Oh, no. Maybe I need one of those spa boosts Bridget is always talking about."

"Or just rest," Pippa said. "You may be Texan, but you're not superhuman."

Eve laughed. "If you say so. I didn't want to ask, but I have a routine medical appointment tomorrow. Can you backup for the nanny?"

It wasn't convenient, but Eve so rarely asked that she couldn't refuse. "No problem. You're sure it's just routine?" she asked.

Eve smiled. "Nothing else. Thank you. I knew I could count on you. But Stefan and I were talking the other night and we both realized how much you do for all the nieces and nephews. You're due some happy times of your own and we're going to work on that."

"Work?" Pippa echoed, fighting a sliver of panic. She definitely did not want to become the object of her family's attention. Especially now. "How?"

Eve shot her a sly look that frightened her. "You'll find out soon enough."

"There's no need to work that hard," Pippa said. "I'm busy with my dissertation and—"

"Don't worry. Just enjoy," Eve said.

"Right," Pippa said nervously. "Don't work too hard."

Eve opened the door to Stephenia's room where the three-year-old sat playing with her toys. "Steffie, I thought you wanted Pippa to read to you tonight. You're not in bed."

Stephenia immediately crawled into bed with an innocent expression on her face, her ringlet curls bouncing against her flushed cheeks. "I'm in bed," she said in her tiny voice, which never failed to make Pippa's heart twist.

Eve tossed a sideways glance at Pippa and whispered, "She's such a heart stealer. We're so screwed."

Pippa laughed under her breath. "Thank goodness Stefan has you. I'm lucky. She'll fall asleep by the time I finish the second book."

"Or first," Eve said in a low voice. "She's been a Tazmanian devil today. I have to believe she's spent some of her energy."

Stephenia lifted her arms. "Mamaeve."

Pippa knew Eve had felt reluctant to take on the name of Stephenia's mother even though the woman had perished in a boating accident. Out of respect, Eve had taught the child *Mamaeve*. Eve rushed toward the child and enveloped her in a loving hug.

"Daddy?" Stephenia asked.

"In the shower," Eve said. "He'll kiss you good-night, but you may already be asleep."

Steffie sighed and gave Eve an extra hug. The sight was heartwarming to Pippa because she'd mostly been raised by hired nannies. She knew it could have been much worse, but it gave her such relief to know that her nieces and nephews would have such a different life than she'd experienced.

"Pippa," Stephenia said, extending her arms, and it occurred to Pippa that she would fight an army to get to her niece.

"I'll let you two go to *Where the Wild Things Are,*" Eve said, backing toward the door and giving a little wave. "Sweet dreams."

"Good night," Pippa said.

"'Night Mamaeve."

Eve smiled and left the room closing the door behind her.

Pippa sank onto Stephenia's twin bed and pulled the child against her. *Where the Wild Things Are* was especially appropriate for Stephenia because the child had been such a bloody screamer when she'd first arrived at the palace. Stephenia was the product of a relationship between her brother Stefan and a model who'd never bothered to tell Stefan about his child. He'd only learned about Stephenia after the mother's death. It had been a shock to the family and the country of Chantaine, but everyone had taken Stephenia into their hearts. How could they not? She had Stefan's eyes and spirit and she was beautiful.

Pippa began to read the book and before she was halfway through, Stephenia was slumped against her, sleeping. She felt the warmth of sleepy drool on her shirt underneath the child's face. Pippa chuckled to herself and carefully situated Stephenia onto the bed. She brushed a kiss onto her niece's head and slid out of the bed, leaving the book on the nightstand. Pippa turned off the light and kissed Stephenia once more, then quietly left the room.

As she walked down the hall, she wondered, not for the first time, if or when she would have children of her own. Pippa knew she'd been shielded from normal relationships with the opposite sex. Every date, and there'd been few, had to be vetted by Stefan, the advisers and of course, security. The only relationship she'd had that approached normality had been her brief *thing* with Nic. She supposed she couldn't really call it an affair because they hadn't done the deed, but Nic hadn't bowed to her unless he'd been joking. He'd treated her like a desirable woman. Pippa couldn't remember another time when she'd felt genuinely desirable.

She rolled her eyes at herself as she entered her small suite. She had far more important things to do than worry about feeling desirable. Thinking back to what Eve had said about how she and Stefan were planning to work on her happiness, she cringed. This was *not* the time.

Nic moved his parents into the cottage. The activity exhausted both of them, so they were taking naps, his mom using her oxygen. She'd begun to use it every night. Nic had adjusted the bed so that her head would be elevated. Many days his mother hid her illness well, but lately he could tell she'd had a harder time of it. She resisted taking too much pain medication, complaining that it made her sleepy. Amelie was determined to get every drop of life she could, and she was giving Nic a few lessons he hadn't expected along the way.

He'd brought over a few members of his crew to clean the pool and jacuzzi and get them operational as soon as possible. He dug into the labor with his men, hoping that expending physical energy would help relieve some of his frustration. Even though he mentally knew that he couldn't make his mother well, he had a bunch of crazy feelings that he spent a lot of effort denying. It was important that he continue that denial because his parents sure as hell had enough on their own plates without his crap.

As he cleaned the side of the pool wall with a brush, he spotted Pippa coming through the gate carrying a bag. She was wearing a skirt that fluttered around her knees and a lacy cotton blouse. As usual, her wild hair was pulled into a topknot. He'd always thought her hair was a sign that she wasn't nearly as proper as she seemed. He knew she considered herself the plainest of the Devereaux sisters, but during that brief period they'd spent time together, he sure had enjoyed making her fair skin blush with embarrassment or pleasure. She was the most sincere and sweetest woman he'd ever met.

Appearing intent on her plan, whatever that was, she walked right past him as if she didn't see him. Just as she lifted her hand to the door to knock, he gave a loud wolf whistle.

His men stopped their work and gaped at him. Pippa stood stock-still, then lifted her hand again to knock. "Hey, PD," he called, climbing out of the pool. "What's the rush?"

Hearing his voice, she whirled around to look at him. "I didn't see you." She glanced at the pool. "You were working?" she said as if such a thought was impossible.

"Yes, I pitch in with manual labor every now and then. It's good for the soul, if I have one, and it usually helps me get a good night's sleep." He liked the way her gaze skimmed over his shoulders and chest, then as if she realized, she was looking where she shouldn't, her gaze fastened on his nose. "My parents are both taking naps. They're worn out from the move."

"It's already done," she said. "You move quickly."

"When it's necessary," he said, thinking perhaps he'd given Pippa too much wiggle room all those months ago.

The door suddenly opened and his mother, wiping

sleep from her eyes, blinked at the sunlight. "What—" She broke off when she saw Pippa and her lips lifted in a smile. "Well, hello, fairy princess," she said.

"Mom," Nic said. "Don't use the P word. Remember this is all on the down low."

"Oh, sorry," she said with a delicate wince. "I'm just so grateful and you made it happen with the snap of your fingers."

"My cousins made it easy," Pippa said.

"But you made the call," Nic's mother said. "I must leave them something in my will."

Pippa bit her lip.

"TMI, Mom," Nic said. "What's in the bag?" he asked Pippa.

"Gelato," she said. "I know we got ice cream yesterday, but this is from one of our favorite gelaterias."

"Let me think of the name," his mother said. "It's on the tip of my tongue."

Pippa opened her mouth, then closed it.

His mother's eyes widened. "Henri's."

"Yes," Pippa said, clearly thrilled. "You have a great memory."

"Bet you brought hazelnut chocolate," his mother said.

"Yes, and a new flavor from the States. Rocky Road. It has marshmallows, chocolate and nuts. Worth a try," Pippa said with a shrug.

"I'll say," his mom said. "Let's taste it now or I'll have to fight the mister for that one."

Nic chuckled at the interchange between his mother and Pippa.

"What are you laughing at?" his mother asked. "Be careful or you'll get no gelato."

"No gelato for me. Water now and beer later," he said.

"Spoil sport," his mother said and he guided Pippa and his mother inside the house.

"I didn't know you were going to fill the pool," his mother said. "Could be a waste," she warned.

"If you enjoy it once, it won't be," he said, heading toward the kitchen. "If you enjoy thinking about taking a dip in the pool or Jacuzzi, then that's enough, Mom," he called over his shoulder as he went to the kitchen and grabbed a bottle of water.

"You're such a good son," she said.

"Does that mean I get some of that gelato?" he asked as he reentered the room.

"And you are the very devil," she said. "Just like your father."

He glanced at both his mother and Pippa. "And you know I'm not anyone but me," he reminded her.

"True," she said. "But he is a scoundrel," she said to Pippa.

"I agree," Pippa said, her eyes swimming with emotions that reflected the drama of the moment. "Well, I can't stay, and I must confess I thought you might not even move in until tomorrow, but I clearly underestimated your son."

"It's not the first time I've been underestimated," he said, meeting Pippa's gaze.

She gnawed on her lower lip and he felt a tug toward her. He'd made a mistake with that before, but something about her got under his skin. He'd known a few women. Some as beautiful as beauty queens and world-class models. Why did she affect him this way?

"I'll try not to do the same thing again," she said.

He shrugged. "We'll see."

"I want gelato," his mother said.

"Then you shall have gelato," Nic said.

Pippa met his gaze, then looked away and walked to the kitchen. "Let me scoop it for you, Mrs. Lafitte. I hope I didn't overdo the chocolate."

"Call me Amelie," she said as she followed Pippa into the kitchen. "And you can never overdo chocolate."

"That's good to know," Pippa said and searched through several drawers for a scoop. "There we go," she said and dipped a scoop of both flavors into a bowl. "Enjoy," she said with a smile on her face.

She shot an uncertain glance at Nic. "Would you like some?"

"I'll wait until later," he said, noting the way Pippa pressed her lips together.

She nodded. "I should go," Pippa said.

"Oh, no," his mother said. "You just arrived."

"You need to rest. You've had a busy day," Pippa said.

His mother frowned. "Promise you'll return."

"Of course I will," Pippa said. "Don't let your gelato melt."

"You're so right," his mother said and dipped her spoon into the treat.

"I'll walk you to your car," Nic said.

"I can do that myself," she said.

"No," he said and escorted her to the driveway. "You need to know," he told her. "It's going to go down from here. She was good just now, but she's struggling and it's just going to get worse. A lot of people wouldn't be able to handle it…."

She stopped and turned, looking offended. "I'm not a lot of people. I'm not the type of person to abandon someone when—" She broke off and realization crossed her face. "You said that because I broke off our relationship."

He shrugged. "If the shoe fits."

"That was a totally different situation," she said. "It was a temporary flirtation. You and I are not at all well-suited."

"Because your family hates mine," Nic said, feeling a twist of impatience.

"That's part of it. There's no good reason for us to continue a relationship when we know there's no future. It was sheer craziness on my part."

He laughed. "Good to know. You're saying you weren't really attracted to me. You were just temporarily insane."

"I—I didn't say that," she said.

Nic watched the color bloom in her cheeks with entirely too much pleasure.

"And what if my last name was not Lafitte?" he had to ask because the question had dug at him at odd moments.

Her expression changed and a hint of vulnerability deepened her eyes. She opened her mouth, then closed it and looked away. "I can't let my mind consider that because you are who you are. I am who I am." She shook her head and turned toward her vehicle. "I need to leave. I'll check on your mother la—"

Nic saw her foot catch on a tree root and instinctively caught her as she tripped. He pulled her against him and inhaled her soft, feminine scent and felt her body cling to him. For about three seconds. Then she pushed at his arm and moved away from him.

"I should have been watching. Sorry," she said and met his gaze.

"No big deal. You're okay. That's what matters," he said.

In that moment, in her gaze, he saw the same tug and pull of feelings that he had inside him about her, about them. There was so much she wasn't saying that she looked as if she could nearly pop from it. "Thank you," she finally said.

*"Ciao,"* he said and watched her as she got into her car and drove away. There was unfinished business here for both of them, he thought. He'd tried to leave Pippa behind, but something about her nagged at him like a fly in the room he couldn't catch. He needed to find a way to get her out of his system.

That night Pippa dressed for the family dinner her brother Stefan had called. With her youngest brother playing soccer in Spain, and her oldest two sisters and their families out of the country, that left Bridget, her husband, Ryder, the twins and Stefan and Eve and Stephenia. She was extremely bothered from her visit with Nic and his mother this afternoon. Amazing how such a brief time in the man's presence could disrupt her so much. She'd suspected he would get over her in no time. He was far more experienced than she was. There must have been a dozen women ready and willing to soothe his ego.

Yet, he acted as if he was still irritated by the fact that she'd ended things. It wasn't as if she'd truly dumped him. They had never had a public relationship, just a few furtive meetings. She couldn't deny he'd made her knees melt with the way he'd looked at her, and the connection she'd felt with him had made her breathless. She also couldn't deny that he'd acted as if he were attracted to her, as if she meant something to him.

The truth was part of the reason she'd refused to see him again was because her out-of-control feelings frightened her. If ever a man was unsafe, it was Nic Lafitte. Yet she'd found him irresistible which only proved that she must have some sort of self-destructive tendency inside her that she hadn't known existed. Now that she knew she had this tendency, she had to beware of it and fight it if it ever reared its head again.

Pippa looked into the mirror and adjusted her top-knot of out-of-control hair. She called it her curse. Every once in a while, the humidity lowered and her hair was almost controllable. Not today, though. Putting on a little lip gloss, she dismissed it and her other thoughts and headed toward the royal dining room.

Stefan had instigated the "family dinners" a couple years ago. Ever since Bridget had gotten married, she'd felt the odd man out at the dinners. She'd worked around those feelings by focusing on her nephews and niece. But still…

Entering the dining room, she spotted Bridget and Ryder holding the twins while Eve chased Stephenia.

With the three high chairs, the palace looked far different from last year.

"Stefan will be here any minute. No need to put the darlings in the high chairs until then. How was your day?" Eve asked Pippa.

"Good," Pippa lied. "Made a little progress on my research."

"Good," Ryder said as he held Tyler and shifted from foot to foot. "Your genealogy studies could really help me with medical plans for Chantaine. I'm working on health prevention at the moment, and I'd like to see a better developed hospice plan in space."

Pippa's stomach clenched at the mention of hospice, although she wished Amelie could have access to such a program. "Both of those are vital. We're very fortunate Bridget brought you to us."

Bridget held Travis and smiled up at Ryder. "I can't agree with you more," she said as she jiggled the boy. "I hope Stefan doesn't take much longer or this family dinner is going to turn into a family scream-in."

Eve winced. "He said it would be just a moment."

"Yes, but we all know it's tough being crown prince and we're glad he's doing it and not us."

Seconds later, Stefan entered the small room with a broad smile. "You're all here. And healthy. This is good."

"And rare," Bridget added. "Given the twins' on-and-off sniffles. We'd better get on with the family dinner. I can't promise how long they'll last."

"No problem," Stefan said. "Sit down and relax. The food will arrive immediately. My assistant advised the chef."

The small group situated the children and sank into their chairs as staff poured water and wine for the adults and juice for the young ones. Before too much fussing, a server brought Cheerios for the babies.

"Takes them longer to pick up," Eve said with a smile.

"Well done," Bridget said.

"The main course will arrive in just a moment. I'd like to take this moment to share some good news. Eve and I are expecting our first child."

"Second, including Stephenia," Eve added.

"Oh, how wonderful. Another baby," Bridget crowed. "Takes the pressure off me."

Pippa laughed at her sister's reaction. "And me."

Bridget and Eve gasped at the same time. "You wouldn't dare. You're the good sister."

"Oh, no," Bridget corrected herself. "That's what we said about Valentina and she got pregnant before she was married."

"I was just joking," Pippa said.

"Thank you," Stefan said as he lifted his glass of wine and took a hefty sip. "One heart attack at a time, please."

"Besides," Bridget said as the staff served filet of sole. "We have plans for you."

Pippa felt a sliver of nervousness and took a sip of her own wine. "You and Eve keep talking about plans. You're making me uneasy."

"They're good plans," Bridget said as she set a plate of cheese, chicken and vegetables on Tyler's tray.

"We know you've been cooped up working on your degree," Eve added.

"Chantaine has several celebratory events scheduled during the next few weeks," Stefan said.

Pippa took a bite of the perfectly prepared fish.

"And we're going to set you up with some of the most eligible bachelors on the planet," Bridget said gleefully. "How exciting is that?"

Pippa's bite of fish stuck in her throat. "What?"

"It will be fun," Bridget said.

"No pressure," Eve said. "We just want you to enjoy yourself. You work hard with your nephews and niece and your studies."

"It's occurred to me," Stefan said, "that you haven't had many opportunities to form relationships with men. You've been protected. Perhaps overprotected."

Pippa's stomach tightened. "How lovely of you all to decide it's time for me to have a relationship. Without consulting me, of course."

Silence descended over the room. Even the children were silent as they munched on their food.

"We thought this would make you happy," Bridget said. "You work so hard. We wanted you to have some fun."

"Would you want your sisters and brother to make decisions about men you would date?" Pippa challenged.

Bridget winced. "When you put it that way…" she said.

"I am," Pippa said. "I don't need or want you to find dates for me. It's embarrassing," she said, her appetite completely gone.

"We don't intend it to be embarrassing," Stefan said. "Your position in the royal family makes it difficult for you to socialize with men. We'd like to make that easier."

"The same way the advisers tried to make it easy for you," Pippa said, setting down her fork.

"There's no call for that," Stefan said.

"And there's no call for matchmaking for me," Pippa said.

"Pippa, you haven't been the same since the incident with—" Bridget cleared her throat and lowered her voice. "That horrible Nic Lafitte. We just want to help you get over it."

"I'm completely over it. I know he was only interested in me to make a point with his ego." Even as she said the words she knew her family wanted to hear, she felt as if she were stabbing herself. "I may be naive, but I'm not a complete fool." She debated leaving the table, but knew her family would only worry more about her. She lifted her drink. "We have more important things to celebrate. Cheers to Stefan and Eve's new baby. May your pregnancy be smooth and may your child sparkle with the best of both of you."

Ryder lifted his glass. "Here, here."

"Here, here," Bridget said.

Tyler let out a blood-curdling scream, and the tension was broken. Soon enough, Travis joined. Stephenia followed.

Most important the focus was no longer on Pippa. She took another big sip of wine and knew she wouldn't be able to eat one more bite of food. With the children providing a welcome distraction, she gave a discreet signal to one of the servers, who immediately removed her plate. As she looked at each face of her family, she felt a combination of love and sheer and total frustration. She wished she could scream just like Tyler did.

## Chapter Four

Two days later, Pippa mustered the time and courage to visit the Lafittes. The name Lafitte was like pyrotechnics as far as her family was concerned. Perhaps she should mentally give them another name so her stomach didn't clench every time she even thought it. Instead of Lafitte, she could think of them as the LaLas. Much less threatening. No unnecessary baggage with LaLa.

The idea appealed to her and Pippa smiled to herself when she thought about it, which was entirely too often. It was difficult not to become impatient with her sisters and brothers over the feud with the Lafittes. After all, the Lafittes were human, too. Look at their current situation with Amelie trying to make it through her dying days and poor Paul with his broken foot. And poor Nic trying to manage all of it.

Sighing, she pulled into the driveway and stopped the car. She glanced over her shoulder even though she was certain her security guy had been dozing when she'd left. That was Pippa. She knew well how to bore a man to sleep. She glanced in the mirror and bared her teeth at herself.

Grabbing the flowers from the passenger seat, she got out of the car and braced herself for the possibility of seeing Nic in workman mode in a tight T-shirt and slim-fitting jeans. Walking into the courtyard, however, she saw no workers around and the pool and Jacuzzi were full of fresh clean water. The sunlight glinting on the water made it all the more enticing, but she suspected the water was frigid.

The house was so quiet and peaceful she wondered if Amelie and Paul might be napping again. She hesitated as she stood in front of the door, not wanting to disturb their rest.

"Hey."

Pippa turned at the sound of Nic's voice as he walked from the guest quarters closer to the driveway. "Hello," she said. "I was afraid to interrupt. It's so quiet."

"I heard your car in the driveway," he said. "Last I checked both my parents are napping again, although I think my mom is getting restless. She'll need a field trip soon. Nice flowers. Come on inside," he said and opened the door to the cottage. He paused, cocking his head to one side. "I'll check to see if the bedroom door is still closed. Just a minute."

She watched him walk down the hallway. Seconds later, he returned, his face creased with concern. "She's gone."

Pippa bit her lip, feeling a quick spurt of apprehension. She couldn't help remembering how Amelie had fainted the last time she'd gone out on her own. "Are you sure she's not somewhere else in the house? Taking a nice long bath. Maybe she's in the kitchen."

He shook his head as he walked toward the kitchen. "I could see the open door of the bathroom." He glanced in the kitchen. "Not there. This isn't good."

"Maybe she went for a little walk in the neighborhood," Pippa suggested hopefully.

"The problem with my mother is that she doesn't take little walks. She probably escaped when I was working and the new house staff went to the market. I thought she was sleeping," he said and swore under his breath. "I have to go look for her."

"But where?" Pippa asked, watching his muscles bunched with tension even as he rolled his shoulders.

"I don't know, but I can't sit here waiting. I'll leave a note for Dad and Goldie. He'll be helping out here at the cottage for the time being."

Wanting to help, she impulsively offered, "I'll go with you." She suspected she surprised herself as much as she'd surprised him.

He gave the offer a flicker of consideration, then shook his head. "There's nothing you can do. I'll call or text you when I find out anything."

His easy dismissal of her irritated her. "I do know Chantaine better than you do."

"What's to know? The island isn't that big," he said.

"Did you know about Bebe's Crepes?" she asked.

"No, but—" He broke off and raked his hand through his dark hair. "Okay. But my first priority is finding my mother. If you're afraid someone may be able to identify you, you'll just have to duck behind the seat."

"Yes. Just let me put the flowers in water and grab my baseball cap," she said.

"I'll go ahead and call Goldie and ask him to come back now. I don't want my dad freaking out here by himself."

Pippa quickly placed the flowers in a pitcher she filled with water because she couldn't find a vase. Hearing Nic's low voice in the background gave her a sense of urgency. She raced to her car to grab the baseball cap. She'd put her hair in a topknot again, refusing to fight with it this morning. Pulling it down, she looked for an elastic band so she could put it in a ponytail and slip it through the back of the cap.

Hearing Nic's feet on the gravel of the driveway, she glanced up and pushed her fingers through her hair self-consciously.

"You should wear it down more often," he said.

"Oh, so I can look like I put my finger in an electrical socket?" No one had ever pretended to like her hair. She'd heard of a treatment that might tame it, but the idea of the hours it would take to accomplish it put her off.

"I like it," he said with a slow grin. "It's kinda wild. Makes me wonder if you have a wild streak underneath."

"I don't," she assured him and stuffed the unruly mass through the back of the ball cap as best as she could. "Shall we go?"

"I'm ready," he said and tucked her into the passenger side of his Mercedes.

"Has your mother mentioned any particular places in

Chantaine that she wanted to visit?" she asked as soon as Nic pulled out of the driveway.

"Since she moved into the cottage, she's just talked about how happy she is to be here, how beautiful it is."

"Hmm. Where are we headed first?" she asked.

"The beach," he said.

"That's a bit to cover. I don't supposed you've heard her talk about any specific beaches," she said.

"I've heard her talk about Chantaine a lot," he said, narrowing his eyes in deep thought. "She used to tell us bedtime stories about Chantaine before we went to sleep at night when my father was gone."

"Gone?" she asked.

"In prison," he said. "His conviction was overturned on a technicality. For a while there, she wouldn't let him come back."

Shocked by his revelation, she blinked. "I'm sorry. I didn't know. That must have been difficult."

"It was the gift that keeps on giving. My older brothers never forgave him. My younger brother just withdrew."

"But they've been in touch with your mother since she's been ill," she said.

"They won't talk to her if there's any chance they have to speak to my father," he said.

"Oh, my goodness, they're as bad as my family," she blurted. "If not worse."

He shot her a sideways glance, but kept his focus on the road. "Yeah."

"I'm sorry, but I'm just shocked. You never told me about all of this. Of course, I'd heard things about your father from my family, but you just said his conviction was overturned."

"Yeah, well, everyone's got a few skeletons in their closet. Even Stefan with his surprise daughter," he said.

Pippa bit her lip. It had been both scandalous and traumatic for the entire family and country for Stefan to learn he'd fathered a child fifteen months after the fact. "As soon as he'd learned about her, he'd done his fatherly duty. He's been a wonderful improvement over the example he had, let me tell you."

"Does that say more about your father or Stefan?" he challenged.

"My father wasn't involved with us. He procreated so that there would be children to carry on the work of the Devereauxs. The more he procreated, the more he could stay on his yacht and the less he would have to do." Her heart was slamming against her rib cage. She'd thought she'd settled all this as a child. Heaven knew, it was old news. "Stefan *reads* to his daughter most nights."

"Okay, okay," he said. "No need to yell."

"I wasn't yelling," she said, then reviewed her words and felt a slap of embarrassment. "Was I?"

"Just a little, but I probably deserved it," he said and pulled the car alongside the beach. "Let's check here." He opened the door for her and they scanned the beach from each direction.

"Did she mention this as one of her favorite beaches?" she asked, staring past rows of hot bodies.

"No. It's just the closest to the cottage. Why do you ask?"

"Well, Chantaine's beaches may share sand and

water, but they each have their own personalities," she said.

"Such as?"

"This is more of a singles scene, a pickup beach. As you can see from the demographics, a younger crowd frequents this beach. Farther north near the resorts, you'll find the celebrities and international visitors. Even farther north, there's a family beach where you'll see more children."

His hair whipping in the wind, he narrowed his eyes. "What's the name of the family beach?"

"St. Cristophe," she said.

"It was on the tip of my tongue," he said. "Let's go there. She went there often as a child before her parents died. She talked about eating fruit, cheese and crackers at the beach. I just hope she didn't decide to go into the water."

They both got into the car, traveling in silence up the coast. Pippa could sense Nic's tension. "If you could just persuade her to leave a message before she leaves…"

"Tell me something new. Maybe she'll listen to you if you say something to her," he said.

"Me? Why would she listen to me?" she asked, surprised at the suggestion. Amelie had only just met her.

"She's grateful to you for the use of the cottage and you're female. She thinks I'm just being overbearing and protective," he said.

"I'll give it a try," she said, full of doubt. "Maybe we could get a list of things she wants to do."

"Like a bucket list?"

She cringed. "That's morbid."

"But part of the program at this point," he said, clenching his jaw.

Pippa's heart twisted. She hated it for all of them, but Nic was only speaking the truth. "St. Cristophe Beach is just a few more kilometers north. We should be there soon."

As soon as the sign for the beach greeted them, Nic again pulled onto the side of the road and helped her from the car. Pippa scanned the beach. "Do you see her?"

He shook his head. "Let's split up. I'll go south. You go north. Call my cell if you find her and I'll do the same. Okay?"

She nodded in agreement and walked northward. The breeze was picking up and the clouds were rolling in, bringing the air temperature down. With Amelie's slight frame, Pippa feared the woman could become easily chilled even though it was summer.

Walking along the beach, she looked from one side to the other. Chantaine's beaches had their share of rocks and trees. Going barefoot could lead to serious discomfort. One more thing to worry about if Amelie had impulsively removed her shoes.

"Look! Isn't that Princess Phillipa?" a woman's voice called.

Pippa froze. Bloody hell, now what could she do.

A woman and several children raced toward her. Oh great, her security detail was going to kill her.

"Your Highness," the woman said, making an awkward curtsy. "Boys, take a bow. Girls, curtsy."

Pippa couldn't help smiling at the woman's delight and friendliness. "It's not necessary. I was here just taking a little walk. St. Cristophe is such a lovely beach. Are you enjoying your day?"

"Very much," the woman said.

The children echoed, "Yes, ma'am."

"Even more so seeing you here," the woman said. "Is there any chance you would give me an autograph? It would be a dream come true."

Seeing a small crowd forming, Pippa knew she'd better make the best of it. "Now, I didn't want to make a big production of this, so you're going to keep my little escape to the beach a secret. Won't you?" Fat chance with Facebook and Twitter alive and well.

She began to shake hands, sign autographs and make pleasant conversation. It really wasn't that difficult. The people were so lovely and kind. Her cell phone rang in the small purse she carried. "Excuse me for just a moment," she said and drew back slightly from the crowd.

"I found her," Nic said. "She was sitting beside a tree sleeping."

"I'm so relieved for you," she said. "But I've been discovered. Go ahead and take her home."

"How will you get back?" he asked.

"I'll figure out something. Or someone will alert security and it won't be necessary. I just wish my car wasn't in your driveway."

"I'll have Goldie take care of it. Where do you want it?"

"Close by, but he doesn't have the key."

"Goldie won't need it," he said. "I'll text you when he's close. He'll grab a cab ride back. *Ciao.*"

Pippa opened her mouth to protest, but she knew Nic had hung up, so she turned back to the crowd and continued to chat, sign autographs and even pose for a few photographs. Yes, there was going to be an inquisition in her very near future. Several moments later, her cell signaled a text. Certain it was from Nic, she didn't bother to look and began to say her goodbyes.

"It was lovely meeting all of you," she said. "But I really must go. *Ciao.*"

She climbed the sandy hill to the road and after walking south a short distance, she spotted her vehicle. Unfortunately she also spotted the vehicle belonging to her security man Giles. Dread tightening her stomach, she walked toward the man. She really didn't want to lose Giles as her personal security guard. He was, after all, the oldest security member on the force. With the exception of her secret meetings with Nic nearly a year ago, he regarded her as a sweet but boring student who posed very little security threat. Plus he was given to taking nice long naps in the afternoon.

"Your Highness," he said wearing an extremely displeased expression. "You didn't inform me of your plans to visit the beach today."

"I know," she said. "I'm terribly sorry. It was an impulse after lunch. I mentioned my plans to pop into a café for lunch, didn't I?"

Giles shook his head. "No, ma'am, you didn't."

"Oh, it must have slipped my mind. You know I usually pack a lunch, but I forgot this morning. My recent studies have been a bit depressing, detailing the causes of deaths of all our ancestors. I just felt a walk on a family beach would clear my head," she said, hoping she was boring the bloody stuffing out of him.

"But you usually prefer the more isolated Previn Beach," he said.

"I know. I guess I just wanted to see happy families playing on the beach. I do apologize. I would never want to trouble you."

"I know you wouldn't," he said. "But you must apprise someone of your whereabouts. If something happened to you, I would never forgive myself."

"You are absolutely correct and I'll never do it again," she lied and felt guilty, but she couldn't change the course she'd started and she wouldn't if she could.

"But you should have informed your Giles or someone," Frank, the head of security said to her. Because one interrogation wasn't enough.

"I know," Pippa said. "But I also know that Stefan has said that he wants us to make more impromptu public appearances."

"Impromptu to the public, not to security."

"So sorry," she said, and tried to conceal her insincerity. It seemed to be growing easier. She hoped she wasn't becoming a lying wench.

Frank sighed and began to pace across her public den. "Your Highness, except for your lapse with *Mr. Lafitte,* you have been an easy royal to protect. Since then, your studies and family have dominated your life. We don't wish to intrude, but if you continue to be unpredictable, then we will need to provide further security."

"I apologize again for not giving you more information today. I will do my best to be as predictable as possible in the future," she said.

Frank gave a sideways tilt of his head. "Perhaps I wasn't clear. We need you to be transparent."

Pippa gave a slow nod. The last thing she wanted to be was transparent. "Of course. And that's exactly what I shall be. Transparent. Predictable," she quickly added.

"Thank you very much, Your Highness," Frank said. "It is only our desire to protect you."

"I know," Pippa said. "And I'm very grateful," she added, exaggerating.

Frank smiled and nodded. "Thank you, Your Highness. I knew we could count on you."

Pippa lifted her lips in a smile as he left her suite. She'd just bought herself a couple more days of freedom. She hoped.

The following day, Pippa skipped visiting the Lafittes and even texting Nic. She felt as if she needed to stick to being predictable and transparent for at least one full day. That next night, however, she tossed and turned as she tried to sleep. She couldn't be what she needed to be for her family. She couldn't be what she wanted to be for the Lafittes.

She finally fell into a fitful sleep full of images of Nic and Amelie. Strong, strong Nic who would never admit pain or vulnerability, yet his dark eyes said something far different. Unable to sleep, she paced her bedroom and tried to work. She finally gave in and sent a text to Nic. I'm going to need a different disguise.

When a civilized time of day finally arrived, Pippa took a shower and got ready to go to the library. She sat down to work, and even though she had the concentration of a water newt, she forced herself to focus. Some time later, a package was placed beside her.

Glancing up, Pippa caught sight of a big bald man walking away from her. She lifted her hand. "Sir?"

The man didn't turn around. Pippa frowned, staring at the package. She glanced around her, then turned it over. The package bore the initials PD. Curious, she eyed the package with a sideways glance and slid it onto the chair beside her. Nic Lafitte was crazy. Who knew what scheme he had in his wicked mind?

She glanced back at her own laptop and with her heart racing, she tried to stare at the screen. Forget concentration. She would just like to be able to *read* the words on her screen. After seven tries, she gave up, grabbed the package and walked to the ladies' room. She went into a stall, ripped open the package and pulled out a gray-haired wig. Pippa couldn't help snickering. Her curiosity shooting upward, she pulled out the rest of the contents of the package. A hat, an ugly gray dress, tennis shoes and a key to a car.

She fished out a scrawled note at the bottom of the package. "The car is old, gray and rusty. In America, we call it a POS mobile. More later."

*POS mobile?* She couldn't wait to hear his explanation, she thought as she changed into the ugly gray dress. After she finished dressing, she carefully folded her other clothing and placed it into the package. Walking out of the restroom, she looked into the mirror and gaped. She looked at least thirty years older if not more. Pippa snickered again. *Well done, Nic.*

Following her instincts, she walked out the back door of the library and looked around for an old gray, rusty

car. She immediately spotted it. The car was the most
hideous vehicle she'd ever seen. Pippa walked to it, un-
locked the door and got inside.

She turned the key and pressed the accelerator. The
engine coughed to life. The summer heat combined
with her wig and droopy dress made her feel as if she
were suffocating. Pippa pushed the button for the air-
conditioning, but only hot air blew from the vents.

"Bloody hell," she muttered and drove out of the
parking lot.

Nic heard the sound of an engine backfiring outside
his window. Glancing away from his tablet computer,
he saw a gray-haired woman in a black dress exit the
car and felt a ripple of pleasure. She'd come. He hadn't
been sure she would. Pippa was an odd mix, and he'd
already learned the hard way her first loyalty was to
her family. She'd probably endured some pressure from
her security guy and maybe even her family if they
knew about it.

He was surprised she continued to visit. After all,
her conscience should be clear. She'd made a dying
woman's wish come true. Heading for the door of the
guesthouse, he wondered why Pippa clearly felt the need
to do more.

He stepped outside and caught sight of her walking
toward the back door. "May I help you, miss?" he called,
relishing the opportunity to tease her.

Whirling around with her hands on her hips, she
stared at him, the gray curls of the wig so stiff they
didn't move. "Very funny," she said. "As if you didn't
handpick this lovely disguise."

"It worked, didn't it?" he asked as he strolled toward her.

She gave a reluctant nod. "Yes, but the car is another matter."

"I'll get Goldie to do something about the engine backfiring. We wouldn't want to call attention to you."

"The car may be a little over the top," she said. "It's distinctive and there's no air-conditioning."

"That must be hard on a woman your age," he said and bit back a grin. Lord, he felt like someone had turned on the light for the first time in two days. His mother had been alternately ill and sleeping. "I wasn't sure you'd come."

Her expression of contempt waned slightly. "You made it easy." She sighed. "How is she?"

He shook his head. "Not good. Sick or sleeping for close to thirty-six hours. It seems she gets a burst of energy and uses up all of it, then she can barely lift her head for days. I never know when one of these dips is the beginning of the—" He broke off. "Something bad."

"I'm sorry," she whispered. "I'm really sorry."

Feeling as if he'd revealed too much, he looked away from her and shrugged. "Part of the program. I'll deal with it. Good thing I've got Goldie. He's a licensed practical nurse, too."

Pippa blinked. "Goldie appears to be a man of many skills. Where on earth did you find him?"

"He and my father were in prison together. Goldie's record wasn't expunged, but he was a good guy. I hired him and he developed a hobby of educating himself. I paid for all the courses, but they've ended up benefiting me."

He felt her gaze on her for a long moment.

"I would like to meet him, please," Pippa said. "So far, I've only caught glimpses of his talents and abilities."

His gut tightened with something strange he almost couldn't identify. It took several seconds. Jealousy? He racked his brain to remember when he had felt this way before and couldn't. He led the way to the house. "Sure, I'll introduce you to Goldie. He's in the main house probably putting together a gourmet meal for dinner."

"He's a chef, too?" she asked.

"Oh, yeah, that was another one of his certificates. It's paid off in spades."

"The palace would *love* to have someone like him...."

"Don't even think about it. But if you do, he'll turn you down flat. He's the most loyal ex-con ever," Nic said.

"That remains to be seen," Pippa said. "The Devereauxs have seduced more than a few of the best of the best."

He stopped at the front door and turned around to meet her gaze. "I know that better than most."

Her cheeks heated and her eyes darkened. She cleared her throat. "Um..."

"Yeah, um," he echoed, saving her a response and opened the front door. "Let's go inside."

He guided her past the foyer into the kitchen. "Goldie," he said in a low voice.

The multitalented man appeared within two seconds, wearing an apron around his waist. "Yes, sir."

Goldie was sixty, but looked fifty because he worked

out. He was bald, muscular, with a gold hoop in his right ear. He usually wore a black T-shirt and black pants. He looked intimidating, but Nic knew he had a heart softer than that of a teddy bear. "Her Royal Highness, Princess Pippa Devereaux, this is Gordon Goldwyn."

Goldie gave a solemn bow. "Your Highness, my pleasure," he said.

Pippa smiled. "My pleasure," she said. "You're a man of many talents. Thank you for delivering my car to me at the beach and also leaving the envelope and car for me."

"I'm honored to serve," Goldie said respectfully.

"How is it that you are talented in so many areas?" she asked.

"I'm a lifelong student. Some things I learned got me into trouble. I'm fortunate that Mr. Lafitte encouraged me to explore my interests. Would you care for a drink or something to eat?"

"I'm fine. Thank you very much."

Goldie nodded, then turned to Nic. "Can I get something for you, sir?"

Nic waved his hand. "No, thanks. Any sign of my mother?"

"No, but your father is getting restless watching her," Goldie said.

"You're saying he could use some TV time. Sports Central," Nic said.

Goldie nodded. "A game would be even better."

"I got a million on DVD," he said.

"Then you've got what he needs," Goldie said.

At that moment, his mother walked into the room, looking gray and gaunt. "I'm thirsty," she said.

Nic rushed to her side. "What are you doing?"

She leaned against him. "I'm Lazarus rising from the dead. Hopefully, I'll do it a few more times," she said and stared at Pippa. "You look familiar. Are you someone who went to school with me?"

"Not quite," Pippa said with a smile. "But I would have loved that."

His mother frowned. "Were you in the orphanage with me?"

Pippa shook her head. "No, but you and I went to Bebe's Crepes together."

His mother stared at her for a moment, then smiled. "Princess Pippa," she crowed. "I love the look," she said, stretching out her hands. "You're my old best friend Rosie."

Pippa nodded and he saw that she was holding back her laughter. "Thank you so much. I'm sure Rosie is a most excellent person."

His mother nodded. "She is, but you are, too." Her eyebrows furrowed. "May we please have some refreshments?" she asked.

"What would you like, ma'am?" Goldie asked.

"Something fruity," she said. "Orange juice or lemonade."

"I'll bring both," he said. "Please take a seat in the den."

Nic assisted his mother to sit on the sofa. "There's no need to treat me like an invalid," she complained.

Nic gritted his teeth. Every other day, if not more often, his mother *was* almost an invalid. Yes, he was happy as hell that she didn't want to be treated like one. In his mind, that meant she might be around a little longer.

Pippa put her hand over his and met his gaze as if she knew everything he was feeling. Still dressed as a gray-haired lady wearing a baggy dress, she looked like an angel to him. An angel he wanted more than he'd ever wanted anyone else.

## Chapter Five

Pippa concealed her alarm at how weak Amelie appeared. Just two days ago, she'd seemed an entirely different woman, going off by herself for a jaunt to the beach.

"I want to go on another adventure soon," Amelie announced as she sipped lemonade. "I'd like to go today, but I'm too bloody tired. Tomorrow will be a different story."

Pippa caught sight of Nic rubbing his forehead and face. She could see his shoulders bunch with tension. "Just let someone go with you so we don't have to call out a search team."

"A search team isn't necessary," Amelie said with a stubborn tilt of her chin. "I was fine."

"You were asleep on a public beach. You overestimate your energy level," he said.

She waved her hand in a dismissing gesture. "Plenty

of people doze on the beach. It's one of the pleasures of life. You wouldn't understand because you don't know how to relax."

"If you would agree to a GPS monitoring anklet…"

Amelie's eyes widened in indignation. "I'm not on house arrest. I refuse to be treated like a prisoner during my last days."

"It's just for tracking. Safety. It would give me some peace of mind," Nic added.

"Well, it wouldn't give me peace of mind walking around in public with an anklet designed for criminals."

Nic sighed. "I'm worried about you. What if you collapse and there's no one there to help you? Is that really the way you want to go?"

Pippa cringed at his bluntness, but she could tell he was feeling pressed. She honestly wouldn't like to be in his situation.

Amelie lifted her chin. "I don't get to choose the way I want to go. If it were up to me, I'd transform into a butterfly and float away, but the doctor says that's not possible."

A tense silence followed. Pippa felt it inside her and took a deep breath to ease it. "Well, I can see that the genes for independence and outspokenness are quite strong in both of you. I'm sure both of you enjoy those qualities in each other."

Nic glared at her, but Pippa forced herself to smile. "Mrs. Lafitte, perhaps you and I could go on an outing tomorrow or the next day, depending on how you're feeling. With my new disguise, I believe I'm safe to go anywhere."

Amelie smiled in delight. "Call me Amelie. And you

don't look a thing like yourself. That wig is so horrible, I think you may look even older than I am."

"Thank you," she said and shot Nic a wry look.

"I've been thinking I'd like to learn a new hobby. Years and years ago, I learned to knit, but I've forgotten everything. Do you know of any knitting shops on Chantaine?"

Ignoring Nic's astonished expression, she nodded. "I know of one downtown. If you feel like it, we could also have lunch."

Amelie seemed to brighten at the suggestion. "Lovely. This will be wonderful. I like having something to look forward to." She paused and glanced at Nic. "Have you heard anything from your brothers?"

"No," he said, and Pippa noticed the slight clench of his jaw. "You should let me call them again."

She shook her head. "You did that last year when I had my last treatments and they all visited then. It was a disaster with your father. I was just hoping things could be different now." She sighed. "There are some things we can't change. Best not to focus on them. I'll look forward to my outing with you tomorrow," she said to Pippa. "I think I'll sit outside by the pool with a book and this lovely lemonade."

"It's a beautiful day," Pippa said. "I think you'll enjoy it."

Goldie appeared in the doorway. "Can I get you something to eat?" he asked.

Amelie made a slight face. "If I tell you I'm not hungry, you'll tell me I need to eat something to keep up my strength. Crackers," she said.

Goldie's face fell. He'd clearly hoped her appetite had improved. "Yes, ma'am."

"Are you sure I can't join you outside?" Pippa asked.

"No, thank you, darling. I just want a little Chantaine sunshine," Amelie said and carefully rose from the sofa.

As soon as Amelie left, Pippa turned to Nic. "What is wrong with your brothers? Even my terribly dysfunctional family came together at the end of my parents' lives. Surely your brothers could do the same. It's the only humane, compassionate choice. You must make them come here at once."

Nic leaned toward her and gave a short laugh. "Here's a news flash, Princess. There's no royal decree available for the Lafittes. Besides, we don't respond well to attempted force or manipulation. My older brothers are holding on to a mile-wide grudge against my father. My youngest brother makes sure he's too busy to be contacted."

"But you must have some influence with them," she said, appalled at the situation.

"My oldest brothers would make the trip if they didn't have to face my father," Nic said. "My mother won't allow that. She refuses to turn her back on my dad even though she's earned the right more than once."

Frowning, Pippa rose and paced across the lush burgundy carpet placed on top of the ceramic tile floor. "There's got to be a way. Perhaps Goldie or I could take your father for a drive—"

Nic shook his head. "Not gonna happen. My mother wouldn't allow it."

"Well, we will just have to figure out another way," she said.

"We?" he echoed, rising to walk toward her.

Her stomach dipped as he moved closer. She kept trying to forget his effect on her, but every time she felt she was successful in staying focused on Amelie, Nic did something to upset her equilibrium. Unfortunately, it took very little. Seeing him stand and breathe was apparently problematic for her.

"I'm still not sure why you feel my mother's problems have anything to do with you," he said, looking down at her and resting his hands on his hips.

"Technically, I suppose they don't, but I would think any compassionate person would want to help," she said.

"Including Stefan?"

She bit her lip. "If Eve had anything to say about it, yes, he would help. I know you believe Stefan is a monster, but he's not. Just as he believes you are the very devil, and you're not."

"Good to know you don't think I'm the devil," he said.

She opened her mouth to retract her statement, then decided against it. "I will try to come up with a solution for your mother and your brothers. In the meantime, I can take Amelie shopping tomorrow, but I'll be busy the day after. I'm supposed to escort some soccer player around the island, then accompany him to a charity fundraiser that evening."

He lifted an eyebrow and his eyes glittered with something that gave her pause. "Is that so? Is the fundraiser at the St. Thomas Hall?"

"Yes, as a matter of fact, it is."

"This should be—" His lips twitched. "Fun. I'm invited to the same fundraiser."

"Oh," she said, her stomach taking a downward plunge. "You probably weren't planning to attend, were you?"

"I hadn't decided, but I could use some entertainment. May as well."

"But what about your mother?"

"It will just be for the evening," he said. "Goldie can call me. I'm not glued to Chantaine. I'll have to leave for business commitments within the next couple of weeks." He paused. "I'm at peace with my mother, and she's at peace with me. We have no unfinished business."

Pippa felt the oddest sense of calm and excitement from Nic. She'd never, ever felt that combination before. She took a deep breath and pushed past her feelings of panic about her feelings. That peace Nic had just mentioned, that was what was important. She felt it and knew it deep inside her. "I'm so glad that you have a good relationship with your mother. It will help you after—" She broke off, not wanting to say the words.

"After she's gone," he said.

Pippa nodded slowly.

"Because you didn't have the best relationship with your mother," he said.

"It wasn't horrible," she said quickly. "It was just distant. Our family was different. We weren't raised the way most other children are raised."

"It's different being royal," he said.

She nodded.

He reached out to take her hand in his. His fingers felt strong and sure wrapped around hers. "Most people don't have perfect childhoods. You take the good and screw the bad stuff."

His simple words gave her the biggest rush. They reverberated inside her. She wanted to be that person who could *take the good and screw the bad*. Every once in a while, though, she felt caught between herself as the chubby preteen who didn't feel worthy of her parents' attention and a grown woman who was on her way to earning her doctorate. The touch of his hand just made her want more… At that moment, Nic made her feel she was capable of anything she wanted to do and be.

A loud cough sounded. Mr. Lafitte stood on crutches at the entrance of the room. "Where's Amelie?" he asked, looking more than a little rough around the edges. His hair stuck up in a wild Mohawk and his jaw was heavily whiskered. "Is she okay?"

Pippa automatically pulled her hand from Nic's while Nic turned to his father. "She's fine. Outside by the pool."

Mr. Lafitte slumped forward slightly. "Good. As long as she's not swimming."

Nic winced. "Good point. Goldie," he called, "can you see my mother?"

"She's in a lawn chair, sir."

"Good." Nic took a quick breath. "Can I walk you to your car, Great-Auntie Matilde?"

Pippa felt a flash of realization. She'd forgotten she looked thirty years older. She smothered a laugh at herself. She'd been concerned that she was giving Nic mixed signals.

Well, she would have if she didn't look like his grandmother. Walking out of the cottage, she waved at

Amelie and strode the rest of the way to the horrid vehicle she would drive to the library, where she would
change out of her outfit and return to her identity as
Princess Pippa.

Nic opened the door for her.

"I hope it's cooler now. I burned up on the drive over
here," she said.

"Goldie did a little magic. You should be more comfortable now."

"Thank you," she said.

"Thank you." He leaned toward her slowly and
pressed his mouth just next to hers. It could have been
a kiss on her cheek, but it just missed the mark. It could
have been her mouth, but it wasn't. He almost made her
forget that she was dressed like his grandmother.

Nic watched Pippa putter away in the POS mobile.
She continued to make him admire her. He tried to
name a woman who would be willing to disguise herself as a woman thirty years older and drive a wreck
of an automobile just to check on a dying woman who
was not related to her. Pippa was different. He'd known
that from the beginning.

He returned to the front door.

"Nic, darling, come sit with me for a moment,
please," his mother called. "Ask Goldie to bring you a
Scotch. Or whatever it is that you drink."

"No need," he said. "It's early for that."

His mother glanced up from her wide-brimmed hat.
"Haven't you heard? It's five o'clock somewhere." She
rang the little bell Goldie had given her, insisting that
she ring it anytime she wanted anything.

Goldie immediately appeared. "Yes, Miss Amelie."

"Please fix a drink for Nic. His usual," she said.

Nic sank into the chair beside her. "How's the book?"

"I fell asleep, so I don't know," she said. "But I'm loving the sunshine. You will have many stars in your crown for bringing me to Chantaine."

"That was Pippa's doing," he said.

"And you're quite taken with her," his mother said and sipped her lemonade.

"I wouldn't say that," he said, irritated at her suggestion.

"No, but I'm dying, so I can speak the truth," she said and shot him a knowing glance from the top of her sunglasses. "I would never ever suggest going after a royal especially because Paul and I made a bit of a mess with the Devereauxs back in the day. That said, I can tell the princess is also taken with you."

Goldie delivered his Scotch and Nic took a long drink. "Yes, that's why she dumped me like garbage several months ago."

His mother waved her hand dismissively. "Family's a tricky thing. You ought to know. I'm quite impressed that she's made such an effort to please a dying woman. Especially when her family wouldn't approve. I can't help believing some part of her is trying to help you."

"If so, then that part is buried very deep," Nic said dryly.

"You have to find your own way. I'll just tell you that some people are worth fighting for. Some people are your destiny," she said.

"You're speaking of Dad," he said, always stunned by the fervency of her devotion to his father.

"I am. He would steal for me. He would die for me. He would go to prison for me. He would do anything for me. I hope you'll know that kind of love," she said and leaned back against the chaise longue.

After a lovely lunch and bit of shopping spent with Nic's mother, Pippa prepared herself for her afternoon and evening scheduled with Robert Speight, the world-famous soccer player from England.

"Aren't you excited?" Bridget asked as she *helped* Pippa get ready for an afternoon outing. "He's so hot. Stefan protested. He wanted to put you with a count from Italy, but I insisted. You deserve a treat after all the academic work you've been doing along with being such a good auntie. Good Lord, don't you ever go shopping?" Bridget continued. "All I see are long skirts and blouses."

"I haven't had a lot of time for shopping," Pippa said, wishing she didn't feel such a strong sense of dread about the setup with the soccer player. She feared he was going to be quite disappointed and bored.

"Well, there's always catalogs and online shopping. For that matter, the palace stylist would be happy—" She broke off as she whisked through the hangers of clothing in Pippa's closet. "Don't you even own a cute little pair of shorts?"

"I'm sure there are some in there somewhere. I just prefer skirts. They're more comfortable," Pippa said and reached for a beige linen skirt that flowed to her calves.

"Absolutely not," Bridget said, scooping the skirt back from her. "If you insist on wearing a skirt," she muttered, pushing through a few more hangers. "Ah," she said, pulling out one of Bridget's few above-the-knee skirts. "Here, this one will work."

"I'm not sure it fits anymore," Pippa murmured, holding the pink skirt against her. "And I think I may have stained the blouse that goes with it."

Bridget pulled out a white scoop-neck cotton blouse. "There. It will be perfect with sandals. Why did you cancel the salon appointment I made for you yesterday? I told you about the new treatment. Smooth, shiny hair and because you're Miss Practical, you won't have to spend so much of your time styling it every day."

"I don't spend that much time, now," Pippa said. "I either pull it back or put it on top of my head."

"Hmm," Bridget said and studied Pippa for a long uncomfortable moment. Bridget took her hand and led her to the sitting area of Pippa's suite. "I'm not sensing a lot of enthusiasm about your outing with the soccer player." She sighed. "Please tell me you're not still pining for that terrible Nic Lafitte."

Pippa looked away. "Of course I'm not pining for him. But I'm not pining for a setup, either. Think about it. Did you like it when Stefan set you up with men hoping for a romance or marriage?"

"I hated it," Bridget said. "Fought it with every bit of my strength, but most of those men were at least ten years older than me. Robert is your age. And he's regarded as one of the most eligible bachelors in the world. I'm not trying to arrange a marriage. I just want you to have a little fun. You're due."

Pippa gave a slow nod. "I appreciate the sentiment. You're sweet to want me to have some fun."

Bridget met her gaze and groaned. "But you're not

at all interested. Well, at least give the poor man a try. Trust me when I say I didn't have to do any coaxing to make this happen. He was more than happy to spend the day and evening with you. And who knows? You may have a fabulous time. Promise me you'll *try* to have fun."

"I'll do my best and I'll also try to make sure that Mr. Speight is entertained," Pippa said.

Pippa treated the date as if it were a project. She planned to take the soccer player on a tour of the island, stopping at a few of the famous beaches. If time permitted, she'd arranged for a brief turn on the royal yacht.

Robert Speight was an impressive specimen. He stood over six feet tall with a well-muscled body. His hair was red and skin extremely fair. The exact opposite of Nic, she thought, and immediately wished she hadn't made the comparison. Their date started out well enough with Pippa giving a running commentary on the history of Chantaine as she showed him points of interest. It was only when she saw his head rolling back against the headrest, his eyes closed and his mouth open that she got her first clue that she'd begun to bore the poor man.

Thank goodness she'd arranged for a picnic lunch at a private beach. She and Robert sat on a large blanket and ate food from a gourmet basket prepared by the palace chef. Robert asked for photos, but kept fighting the yawns.

"Sorry," he said sheepishly. "Late night last night partying," he said waggling his bushy red eyebrows suggestively. "If you know what I mean."

She didn't, so she just made a vague little sound. "I

thought it was very generous of you to lend your name to the charity fundraiser this evening. So many people are looking forward to meeting you."

He shrugged. "I have to do a few of these every now and then for the sake of my image. It helps me get other endorsements. This one included exotic beaches and a date with a princess. What's not to like?" He leaned toward her and placed his hand over hers. "I've heard Chantaine has some nude beaches. You want to take me there?"

Pippa blinked at the proposal and tried not to laugh. She'd spent a lifetime trying not to be photographed in a bathing suit. A nude beach was totally out of the question. "I'm not really permitted on the nude beach," she whispered. "Photographs live forever. If you have time tomorrow, I can arrange for a driver to take you."

"But it would be much more enjoyable with you," he said.

"I'm so sorry," she said and took back her hand. She was going to have a chat with Bridget tomorrow, she promised herself.

Later that afternoon, Pippa received a visit from the palace stylist, Peter, to make sure she was properly dressed and coiffed. Dressed in a designer gown that reminded her of a pink cocktail napkin, she bit her teeth. Peter applied more makeup than she wore in a year. He sighed and swore over her hair. "A keratin treatment would change your life."

"It takes too long," she said.

"It's not as if you would have to sit in a salon like the rest of the world. We would bring the cosmetologist to the palace. Your hair would be straight for three to four months after one treatment."

Pippa stared into the mirror at herself and made a face. "I don't know if I want it straight."

Peter lifted one eyebrow. "As you wish, Your Highness."

"Your way of saying I'm crazy," she said.

Both of Peter's eyebrows flew upward, which was quite an accomplishment given the Botox he regularly had injected into his forehead. "Pardon me, Your Highness if I offended you."

"It's true. You think I should get the treatment and have straight hair. Straight hair is more fashionable than crazy, wavy hair."

Peter seemed to work on his restrained. "It's my job to keep the royal family informed of current fashion. Your hair…" He began and moved his hands, but couldn't seem to find the words.

"I hate my hair and love my hair because it's different," she told him. "You have to admit, it's not like anyone else's hair in the family."

Peter tilted his head to one side. "You make an excellent point, Your Highness. We shall begin to capitalize on your hair," he said. "We shall make your hair a new trend. We can name it the Princess Pippa hairstyle. Perfect."

Alarm shot through her. "No need to go that far," she said.

He lifted his hands. "I can see it now. Magazine shoots, commercials. It will be fantastic publicity for the royal family."

"Not in my lifetime," she said quietly.

He sighed. "Begging your pardon, ma'am, you give this impression of being a people pleaser, yet you somehow stop me in my tracks when I try to expand you."

"And you like me for that, don't you, Peter?" she said more than asked, unable to hold back a grin.

Peter shook his head but smiled. "I do. Let me spray you one more time," he said lifting a can of hair spray.

She lifted both her hands to block him. "I'll die if you do."

"An exaggeration," he said.

"You would know because you're the master of exaggeration," she retorted, her hands still braced to shield herself from the hair spray.

Peter groaned. "You make this difficult for me, ma'am. What if this man is your future husband?"

"No worries," she said, adapting a phrase she'd learned from Bridget. "He pushed hard for me to take him to a nude beach."

Peter frowned. "A cad. In that case, perhaps I should give you sea salt spray. It will take your curls to a new level."

Pippa laughed. "No need. Thanks for your help tonight."

"Someday, a man will sweep you off your feet."

Pippa laughed again, and her mind automatically turned to thoughts of Nic. She clamped down her thoughts and feelings. "I prefer my feet on the ground."

Thirty minutes later, she joined Robert Speight in a limo headed for the charity event. "Nice dress," Robert said, staring at her cleavage. "Are you sure I can't talk you into a trip to one of your nude beaches tomorrow?"

Pippa refused to honor the subject, let alone the question. "Did you know that I'm working on a doctorate in genealogical studies? I had some extra time this afternoon while I was waiting on alterations for my gown. Did you know that you may be distantly related to Attila the Hun?" The truth was just about anyone could be distantly related to Attila.

Robert shot her a blank look. "Attila the Hun?" he echoed.

"Yes, he's quite famous."

"I'm drawing a blank," Robert said. "Can you refresh my memory?"

"He was a ferocious warrior. The Romans were terrified of him. He was excellent with a bow and an amazing horseman. Quite the sportsman," she said.

Robert stuck out his chest with pride and smiled. "Like me."

"Exactly. He was known as a conqueror." *And barbarian.*

"I've got to make a little speech tonight. Maybe I could mention him," he said. "Maybe spice things up for people interested in history."

She opened her mouth to correct him, but couldn't quite make herself do it. "Just as long as you understand that I said that you *may* be related to Attila. I would need to do an in-depth study to verify the possibility."

"Hey, it's a good story. That's all that counts to me," he said, leaning toward her as if he were going to kiss her. "You're cute. Let's make some private plans after the event."

"Oh, I—" The limousine pulled to a stop. She glanced out the window, thankful for the interruption. "We're here."

"Yeah," Robert said as the driver opened the door. "First time with a princess. In more ways than one," he added against her ear as he folded his hand around her waist.

Pippa's stomach rolled.

She stepped out of the car and felt a thousand camera flashes as she strode toward the entrance of the building. Robert grabbed her hand and she struggled to free it. She pointed at a camera and she took advantage when he loosened his grip. Clasping her hands firmly together, she walked inside and smiled at the crowd that applauded.

"Pippa, Pippa!"

She was surprised to hear so many call her name. She'd always thought of herself as the anonymous Devereaux.

Robert put his arm around her and whispered in her ear, "Give me a kiss. They'll love it."

She bit her lip and turned her head. "I see some of your fans," she said.

"Where?" he asked.

Moments later, they entered the ballroom and Pippa waved to the crowd. There, several people screamed out loud. "Rob, Rob!"

"There you go," she said, but she needn't have. Robert was fixated on the crowd, waving and throwing kisses.

They were led to the head table and Pippa took her seat. The rest of the guests took their seats. Instinctively, she glanced around and her gaze landed on a man with broad shoulders, dark eyes and dark hair. Tonight he wore that Stetson as if to proclaim to all of Chantaine and her family that he didn't give a damn.

She liked him even more for that.

"This is fun," Robert said. "Just tell me it's not another rubber chicken dinner," he said.

"Lobster," she said and barely managed not to roll her eyes.

She felt Nic's gaze on her. He was silently laughing.

"So that guy's name is Atowla?"

"Attila," she said. "Attila the Hun." She was caught between a barbarian and a pirate. She wasn't sure which was worse.

## Chapter Six

A server discreetly handed Pippa a piece of paper with her sorbet. Putting it in her lap, she opened it and glanced at it. *Meet me on the second floor in 5. N.* Pippa took a quick sip of water and briefly met Nic's gaze. She shook her head.

Her so-called date whispered in her ear. "It's time for more pictures," he said. "Stand up and I'll give you a passionate kiss. The press will love it."

Pippa nearly choked. "I was just going to tell you that I need to, uh, powder my nose. I'll be back shortly."

Robert's face fell. "Well, damn."

"I won't be long," she said and stood. She gave her security man a wave of dismissal and quickly walked to the hall outside the ballroom. Restroom was to the right, she remembered. Pippa had attended several events at this venue. The second floor offered a lovely view of the beach. Her stomach took a dip. Nic clearly remembered that fact, too.

She headed toward the restroom.

"Pippa."

She automatically paused, her heart leaping at the sound of Nic's voice. Pippa sucked in a quick, sharp breath and forced herself not to turn around. She didn't need to because Nic was at her side in seconds. "This is not a good idea. Go away," she whispered.

"Your Highness," a woman called. "Princess Phillipa."

Pippa frowned and turned at the distress in the woman's voice. She stared into the lovely heart-shaped face of a very young-looking woman. She was dressed in a miniskirt and tank top.

"You can't have him. I'm having his baby."

Pippa dropped her jaw. "Pardon me?"

"You can't have Robert. He belongs to me. He's all excited about being with a princess, but it will pass. He'll come back to me. He has to," she said and began to sob.

Pippa instinctively gathered the girl into her arms and glanced searchingly at Nic. "You're getting too upset," she said.

"He belongs to me. I'm having his baby," the young woman continued to sob. "He belongs to me."

"Darling, I wouldn't dream of taking Robert from you. This was just a charity appearance for both of us."

The girl pulled back, her baby blues filled with tears. "But he was so excited about being with a princess. He told me he couldn't make a commitment. Big things were coming in his future," she said, her voice fading to another sob. The woman buried her face in Pippa's shoulder again.

She met Nic's gaze again. "Please ask a server to give Robert a note. Robert's friend and I will be upstairs. He should join us immediately."

Nic lifted a dark eyebrow and dipped his head. "As you wish, Your Highness."

As soon as he turned away, she felt a rush of relief. "Let's go upstairs," she said. "I didn't hear your name."

"Chloe," she said and sniffed and swiped at her cheeks as Pippa led the way upstairs. "You're much nicer than I thought you would be. I was sure you would steal Robert from me."

"Oh, Chloe, I wouldn't dream of that," she said with complete and total honesty. She wouldn't take Robert if he was handed to her on a silver platter. She guided Chloe into a room and propped open the door.

Just a couple moments later, she heard voices coming from the hall. Nic's and Robert's. The door swung open and Nic and Robert stepped inside.

Robert's eyes widened. "Chloe, what are you doing here?"

Chloe bit her lip. "How could you leave me, Robert?"

Looking incredibly awkward, Robert shrugged his wide shoulders. "It was just temporary." He shot a quick glance at Pippa. "The princess required my presence for the charity event."

"I did not," Pippa said, unable to contain herself. She wanted to punch the scoundrel. She clenched her fists.

"Okay, well, I had to show for the charity event. The princess was just a bonus," he amended.

Nic cleared his throat. "I think Chloe has some important news to share."

Chloe gulped and appeared to force a smile. "I'm having your baby," she said.

Pippa looked at Robert and saw the tall, strong athlete turn as pale as ghost. "Baby?" he echoed.

"Yes, I'm having your baby," Chloe said and walked toward him.

Robert fainted backward. Nic caught him just before he would have hit the floor.

Pippa sighed, crossing her arms over her chest. "Are we going to have to call the medics, too?"

"Let's try something a little more basic," Nic said. "Can you get a glass of water?"

She glanced around the room and saw a stack of paper cups and pointed at them. "There's a water fountain in the hall."

"I'll take care of it," Chloe said.

"Get two cups," Nic said and gently lowered Robert's head to the carpeted floor.

Chloe ran out of the room. Seconds later, she returned.

"I think you should have the honors," he said to Chloe.

"What do you mean?" she asked, clearly confused.

"Throw the water in his face," he said.

Chloe's eyes widened in alarm. "In his face."

"It's the best thing for him," he said.

"Are you sure?"

"Couldn't be more sure," he said. "If you don't do it, then I will."

Chloe took a deep breath and threw a cup in Robert's face.

The athlete blinked and shook his head.

"It worked," Chloe said with a delighted smile. "You were right."

Nic nodded and extended his hand. "Can you give me the second cup?"

"Of course," she said and gave it to him.

"You coming around, Speight?" Nic said as the man lifted his head.

"Yeah," he said, rubbing his hand over his face. "Why am I wet?"

"So many reasons," Nic said. "You okay? Are you conscious?"

Robert lifted himself up on his elbows. "Yeah, I'm good."

Nic nodded and dumped the second cup of water on Robert's head.

Robert scowled and swore. "Why the hell did you do that?"

"In Texas we would say you need a good scrubbin'," he said in his Texas drawl. "I just thought I'd get you started. Pops."

After Robert pulled himself back together and dried himself with some paper towels, he returned to the ballroom and Nic arranged for a car to take Chloe back to her hotel.

Pippa felt the pressure of passing time. She knew her absence would be noted if she didn't return soon, but she wanted to thank Nic for his help. After stepping just outside the door, he returned and strode toward her.

"You okay?" he asked, his dark gaze intent on her.

She laughed. "Of course I'm fine, thank you. I wasn't the least bit enamored of Robert from the beginning."

Nic walked closer. "Are you sure about that?"

Pippa frowned. "Of course I'm sure. Do you really think I could be so easily won over by a man just because he's a world-famous soccer player?"

"You fell for me pretty quickly in the beginning," he said, lowering his mouth to half a breath away from hers.

Her heart skipped. "I was young and foolish."

He laughed, and the deep, hearty sound echoed inside her, making her feel alive. "It was six months ago."

"Eight months," she corrected.

He lifted a brow. "I didn't know you were counting."

She opened her mouth, but at the moment, she couldn't deny… Anything.

His mouth brushed hers, and the sensation made her felt as if she were melting and blooming at the same time. His mouth searched, plundered and empowered hers. She felt sensual, womanly, and it sounded crazy, but she felt as if she could fly. It was such an amazing, euphoric sensation that she didn't want it to ever end. During a moment that felt like centuries or seconds, she slid her arms around Nic and reveled in the strength of his body. It seemed to flow into hers.

She craved more of the feeling. There was more, she thought. More…

Nic pulled back slightly. "Let me take you away," he whispered. "For just a while."

Every fiber of her wanted to say yes, but her duty and obligation screamed no. "I want—" She took a breath and tried to clear her head. "They're expecting me for the end of the dinner. After twelve minutes, people start to notice when a royal is gone." She swallowed over the craziness rolling through her, but she fought the drowning sensation she felt when she stared into his eyes. "They actually notice before that, but if there's a distraction such as a famous soccer player, we get a bit more time."

"After the dinner, then," he said.

Her stomach dipped as if her amusement park ride had abruptly plunged and risen and plunged again. "Oh," she said. "Uh, I—" She broke off and shook her head. "This is crazy. We tried it before. It didn't work out."

"Why?" he asked, his gaze wrapping around hers and holding it.

She opened her mouth to answer, but the words stopped in her throat.

"What's the problem, Princess Pippa? Cat got your tongue?" he asked and kissed her again.

Pippa melted again, feeling as if she were having an out-of-body experience. His arms felt better than chocolate, his mouth, the same. She felt as powerful as the ocean. She clung to him, but duty tugged at her. It was so ingrained that she couldn't quite forget it.

Pippa pulled back. "I have to go."

"Chicken," he said.

Something inside her wanted to prove him wrong. "Blast you," she whispered, and wiped her mouth as she ran from the room.

Although she was bloody distracted, Pippa finished the interminable evening. With photos, but no passionate kisses. She took a separate limo to return to the palace, all the while consumed with thoughts of Nic. What if she could have met him? Where? She felt a terrible aching need to be with him, but she knew she couldn't. For a thousand reasons. She arrived to find Bridget waiting in her quarters, bouncing with excitement.

"Tell me all about it," Bridget said. "How hot was he?"

"Too hot for me, given the fact that a, he pushed to go to a nude beach."

Bridget's jaw dropped.

"B, he wanted to French kiss me in public for the sake of getting photographs with a princess."

"Oh, my—"

"And c, congratulations are in order. The very young mother of his baby showed up at the charity event."

"He has a child?" Bridget asked, her eyes wide with horror and shock.

"He is a father-to-be. I believe the popular term is baby daddy."

Bridget gave an expression of pure disgust. "Oh, how horrible. I don't know what to say."

"Just say you won't set me up again," Pippa said. "Please."

Bridget winced. "I'm so sorry." She lifted her hands. "I just wanted you to have a little fun."

"I know your intentions were good," Pippa said. "They always are. You have a good heart and you love me. I know you love me. I just need to find my own way in this area." She decided to make a bigger push. It was her moment. "As you know, my birthday is right around the corner. Everyone is pushing for the palace to make budget cuts. I've decided I want a little more control over where I go. I'm going to request more limited security."

Bridget shook her head, fear filling her eyes. "Oh, no, you can't do that. Not after what almost happened to me. Not after what happened to Eve."

"If you recall, you actually had security when you were leaving that charity event when you were almost stampeded by that gang. I think it makes sense to follow what other royal families are doing. I'm *way* down the list to take the throne and heaven knows I have no interest. Current practices suggest I be given security for official events with a panic button for my use at all times. Do you know how much the head of security grilled me because I took a walk on a family beach last week?"

"It's the social media," Bridget said. "People with camera phones are everywhere, tweeting, taking photos. You can't possibly expect anonymity or privacy, Phillipa."

"It doesn't help to have security nipping at my heels every minute," Pippa said.

"I thought you had a soft spot for your security man. You seemed to have an easy enough relationship with Giles before, well—" Bridget broke off. "Before the Lafitte incident."

Pippa felt her irritation grow. In the past, she would have just sighed and fallen silent. "All of you made entirely too much of a fuss. Can you honestly say you never dated someone Stefan would have considered inappropriate?"

"Stefan considers any man he doesn't choose to be inappropriate," Bridget scoffed and began to pace.

"He almost didn't approve of Ryder until he figured out Ryder could be the new health minister. But Lafitte was different. His family—" Bridget shook her head. "There's just too much bad history between his family and ours. Plus his father had to have been a terrible influence on him."

"Some people might say the same about the influence our father had on us," Pippa muttered.

Bridget shot her a sharp look. "What are you saying?"

"I'm saying I want my personal business to be my business. I'm saying I want to make my own decisions about security and dating."

"We just all adore you and we don't want you to be hurt," Bridget said.

"I realize that, but I'm not four years old. I'm a grown woman. I may be the youngest daughter, but I don't need all of you looking after everything in my life. I want you, Tina and Stefan to stop it. Now." She barely kept herself from stomping her foot for emphasis.

Bridget blinked, then sighed. "You may be able to persuade Tina and me, but good luck with Stefan."

It was a good thing she didn't care what the tabloids said about her, because she would have become extremely depressed the following day. Princess Phillipa Dumped by Soccer Player the headline read with photos from the charity event and her impromptu visit last week on the beach. Not cover-girl shots. Pippa had always shrunk from any potential emphasis of her image. She was no fashion leader, that was certain. Her sisters Fredericka and Bridget had seemed to do enough of that for everyone, thank goodness. It had taken the focus off her. Her other sister, Valentina, had been a bit less fashionable, more normal in her figure and ultimately more concerned with relationships than her image.

That was probably the reason the weight of royal appearances had worn heavy on Tina's shoulders and she'd become the wife of a Texas businessman rancher. Tina made occasional appearances for the family and attended to a few royal duties, but her focus was happily fixed on her marriage and young daughter. Over the years, Pippa had filled in the gaps on the schedule or substituted when one of her siblings couldn't make an event.

She hadn't spent a lot of time thinking about what she truly wanted for herself because she'd been so busy finding ways to avoid causing trouble or being in the spotlight. Ever since she'd gotten involved with Nic all those months ago, she found herself fighting a restlessness that seemed to grow worse every day. She wished it would go away. She'd thought once she'd broken off with Nic that she could go back to normal, but normal didn't fit anymore. Sipping a cup of tea and sitting inside the small suite where she'd lived since she was a teen, she stared outside her window to one of the palace courtyards and felt like a caged bird. She didn't like the feeling at all.

Taking a deep breath, she prepared herself for her meeting with her brother Stefan. He'd requested the meeting first thing this morning. She suspected he had something on his mind and she intended to do what she'd heard Eve say on more than one occasion. Pippa was going to give her brother, the crown prince of Chantaine, a piece of *her* mind.

She walked down the long hallway to the opposite wing of the palace, then up the stairs to the office where her brother worked. On rare occasions, her father had also worked here.

Her brother was a working prince and he'd spent most of his adult life living down their father's yachting playboy prince image. All the Devereaux children had been raised to understand that duty was first and foremost. Some had accepted the duty more easily than others.

Pippa lifted her hand to knock on the door.

Stefan's assistant immediately responded with a slight bow. "Good morning, Your Highness. His Highness is ready for you."

"Thank you," she said and walked through the outer office into Stefan's office.

Stefan stood and smiled. "Thank you for coming on such short notice," he said and moved from behind his desk to embrace her.

Pippa hugged him in return, noting he wore a suit, signaling he had other official meetings today. "As if you would let me refuse you," Pippa gently teased him, taking in the office. The decor combined the history of the Devereauxs with Stefan's interests in horses, his studies in leadership and economics and a few of Eve's homey touches from Texas.

She also noticed a wooden toy on the corner of his desk and pointed at it. "For Stephenia?" she asked, smiling as she thought of his toddler daughter.

"Eve and the nanny bring her to visit. I like to have

at least a couple things in the room that she's allowed to touch. I don't want her to remember my office as the no-no room," he said.

"I like that," Pippa said. "It's a lot different than the way we were raised."

Stefan nodded. "That's the plan. Please have a seat."

Pippa sat on the edge of one of the leather chairs. She would have preferred to remain standing. Standing somehow made her feel stronger. "How is Eve?" she asked.

His eyes lit at the mention of his wife's name. "A bit of nausea and I think she's more tired than usual, but she's trying not to let me see it. I've asked her assistant to limit the number of invitations she accepts. We'll see how long that works. She can be as stubborn as—" He broke off. "As I am."

Pippa laughed. "One of the many things we love about her."

Stefan nodded, then turned serious and she could tell he was going to start discussing the reason he'd invited her to his office. "I'd like to go first, please," she said breathlessly.

His eyes flickered in surprise and he paused a half beat, then gave a slow nod. "All right. Go ahead."

Pippa took a teeny, tiny breath and clenched her hands together. "My birthday is next week," she said.

Stefan smiled. "I know. That was part of the reason I asked you here."

"Really," she said. "Well, I've been thinking about this a lot and I believe I'm ready to drop my security back to official events only."

Stefan stared, again in surprise.

"It's really the current trend among royals and I know you're trying to keep us up-to-date. All of our expenses are being scrutinized by the government and the press, and I think it would be an excellent way to show that we can be economical."

Pippa sat back and waited for Stefan to respond.

"I'll take it under advisement. However, my first response is no. With the brawl Bridget and Eve faced last year, we've learned that we can't count on all our citizens behaving in a welcoming or even civil manner."

"If you'll recall, that was an official event and security was present."

His eyes narrowed with irritation and dark memories. Pippa understood the dark memories. Stefan had been falling in love with Eve when she'd been injured. "I said I would take it under advisement, but you must understand that I regard your protection as a very serious responsibility."

"I appreciate that very much," she said. "But I'm insisting."

He tilted his head to one side in shock. "Pardon me?"

Pippa's stomach clenched. She knew that expression. He'd used it far more often with Bridget because her older sister had felt perfectly free to argue with Stefan. Pippa, on the other hand, avoided arguments like the plague. Except this time.

"I said I'm insisting. I don't do a lot of insisting, but I am this time. And I think you should also know I'm considering moving out of the palace."

Another shocked silence stretched between her and her brother.

"And how do you plan to pay for this apartment?" he challenged.

"I earn a small stipend with the research I do, and I have a savings account. It's true most of my clothes have been provided by the palace, but I don't need a different dress every day. It's not as if everyone is watching every move I make."

"You underestimate how interested our people are in you," he said. "As evidenced by the crowd you drew during your impulsive walk on the beach last week."

Pippa winced. She wondered who had ratted on her. It wasn't as if Stefan spent a lot of time on internet social sites. "Yes, and everyone was perfectly polite."

"You'll be entirely too vulnerable if you were to move away from the palace," he said.

"Entirely too vulnerable to what? I would still have a panic button and I could have alarms set up in an apartment. Admit it. Jacques will be of age soon enough and you would allow him to live away from the palace."

"That's different," Stefan said. "He'll be a young man and would feel trapped here."

"The same way I feel trapped," Pippa said.

Stefan looked as if he'd been slapped and she felt a stab of regret. "I thought you liked having access to the family, the twins and Stephenia, the family dinners."

"I do," she said. "I love my nieces and nephews. I love my family. There's no reason I still can't babysit and attend family dinners. I just need some space."

Stefan sighed, then straightened his shoulders. "Perhaps you just need a break. When I tell you what I have planned for you, I know you'll be pleased."

Pippa felt her stomach twist with dread. There was

always a catch involved when Stefan had a *plan*. "No, really," she began.

He held up his hand. "You've had your turn. Now it's mine. I've arranged for you to take a holiday to the coast of Italy for your birthday."

Pippa immediately thought of Amelie and shook her head. "That's a lovely thought, but this isn't a good time for me to take a holiday. Due to my studies," she added.

"It's only for a few days and the break will be good for you. You'll have only two appearances to make during your trip. One celebrating the anniversary of a museum and the other will be a christening ceremony for a new cruise ship that will be making stops in Chantaine. I've arranged for an escort for you. Count Salvatore Bianchi. He's a bit older than you, but his family is considering opening several wineshops here, so we'd like to further that relationship. And who knows? Perhaps the two of you will hit it off," Stefan said, wearing his most charming smile.

Pippa felt a twist of suspicion. "Just how much older is Count Bianchi?"

Stefan shrugged. "I'm not sure. He's a widow with children. I believe one of them goes to school with Jacques." Jacques, her nineteen-year-old brother.

"So what you're saying is he could be my father," Pippa said.

"Age is just a number, Pippa. I assure you that you'll have more in common with the count than the soccer player Bridget arranged as your escort. My assistant will give you your itinerary later today and the palace stylist will help you with your attire for the trip."

"And if I don't want to go?" Pippa said.

"The arrangements have been made. People will be expecting you. Besides, I can tell by our discussion today that you need this holiday. You *will* enjoy it," he said and stood.

"Because His Royal Highness decreed it," she muttered and also rose.

A flicker of irritation passed over Stefan's face. "I've always counted on you for your sweetness."

She felt a quick surge of pain at the prospect of disappointing Stefan. "I'm sorry. I'll go on the trip, but Stefan you need to understand that it won't change my intentions regarding my security and moving out."

"We'll see," he said.

## Chapter Seven

Two days later, Pippa managed to make her way to the Lafittes' temporary cottage. She drove the rickety car from the library wearing the terrible disguise over her clothes and pulled off the wig as soon as she pulled into the cottage driveway. Unbuttoning the too-large matronly blouse, she stepped out of the car and pushed down the hideous skirt.

She heard a wolf whistle and glanced up to see Nic smiling at her as he leaned against the guest quarters door wearing jeans and a black T-shirt that outlined his broad shoulders and muscular arms. "Don't stop now," he said, referring to her awkward striptease.

She bundled up the disguise in her arms and rolled her eyes as she walked toward him. "I despise this outfit."

"But it gets the job done," he said.

Unable to argue his point, she pushed open the gate. "How is your mother?" she asked.

"Restless. She may need an outing," he said. "A short one. Any ideas?"

"I'll think of something. Have you made any headway with your brothers?"

"Heard from one and I'm hounding the others. I may have to resort to unconventional methods of getting their attention."

She shot a sharp glance at him and he shook his head. "You don't want to know."

"Actually, I do," she said. "I may need to use subversive tactics with my own family at some point."

She felt his glance at her, but didn't meet his gaze. "Okay. I'll send a fake officer to stop them on their way to work. This officer will deliver a message."

She met his gaze. "That's drastic."

Nic shrugged. "Drastic times…"

She couldn't help smiling at his creativity. "Well done."

He shot her a half grin. "It's only the first step. I have others planned if this doesn't work."

She nodded. "What are we doing with Amelie this afternoon?"

"I don't know. Depends on her mood."

"How is her appetite?"

"Temperamental at best," he said.

"Maybe she'll take a few bites of gelato."

"You'll have to put on your disguise again," he reminded her.

"I know. I want to cool off until then."

Nic opened the door for her and she stepped inside

the cool foyer. Pippa walked toward the den and saw Amelie and Paul cuddling on the sofa and watching television. She hesitated to interrupt, but Paul glanced up at her.

"Hey, y'all come on in," he said.

Amelie glanced up at her. "It's Pippa!"

The delight in Amelie's voice grabbed at her heart. "Yes, I'm here for just a while."

"We should have another adventure," Amelie said.

Nic gave a low groan from behind her.

Pippa smothered a smile. "We should plan something."

"I want to do something now," Amelie said. "Paul is feeling better tonight."

Pippa remembered her earlier suggestion. "Would you like some gelato?"

Amelie's face lit up. "Perfect." She turned to Paul. "Do you think you can manage a ride in the car?"

"I can do anything for you," Paul said. "And gelato sounds good, too," he said with a rough chuckle.

Pippa's heart twisted at the obvious love that flowed between the two of them. Reluctantly, she put on her costume again. The four of them got into Goldie's SUV and drove to Chantaine's best gelato shop. They ordered ten flavors. Amelie took a teeny bite of each of them. When they returned, both Amelie and Paul were worn out.

Pippa stripped off her disguise again. "I hate this disguise," she muttered to Nic as they sat by the pool. "I think I hated it from the beginning," she said. "Do you think your mother enjoyed the outing?"

He nodded. "My father did, too. They won't admit it, but it helps if the trip is a short one."

"How do you think your father is dealing with your mother's illness?" she asked.

"Depends on the day. Sometimes he's in denial. Other days he's trying to grab the moment. He's definitely not fit for making business decisions."

"So you're doing that for him?" she asked.

He nodded, his head still resting against the chair, his eyes closed.

"He's lucky to have you stepping in for him," she said.

"Someone has to," Nic said.

She stared at Nic as he sat in the chair, in his jeans and T-shirt, his head tilted back. "But why you?" she asked.

He cracked open an eyelid. "Because no one else would."

"Does that mean you would have preferred to let one of your brothers take on this challenge?"

"I would have preferred to have just about anyone take on the challenge, but I knew no one would. My father is an ex-con. Trust in his business is precarious at best. I have to both check behind him and authenticate his company to his customers."

"If his business is so precarious, how are your mother and he surviving so well?"

Silence settled between them, making Pippa wonder about the mysteries of Nic's family. Suddenly, it dawned on her. "You're taking care of them, aren't you?"

Nic sighed. "His business has huge potential, but with the economy and his reputation, it's a struggle."

Pippa thought about all Nic was trying to do for his parents and felt an overwhelming sense of admiration and something deeper, something she couldn't quite name, for Nic. "You're quite the amazing son."

"You would do the same in my circumstance," he said.

Pippa shook her head. "I wouldn't know how to do everything you're doing," she protested. "Plus my relationship with my parents wasn't half what yours is."

Nic pulled his head from the back of the chair and met her gaze. "But you were there at the end."

Pippa took a deep breath, remembering both of her parents' deaths, and nodded. "Most of us were. Stefan and Valentina pulled us together. It wasn't easy. I think they suffered because of it."

Nic nodded. "It's a tough time. If there are more people, there's a bigger cushion."

"But you have none," she said.

He shrugged and cracked a grin. "I'm from tough stock. We've had to scrabble for everything. No royalty in my blood."

"Hmm," she said. "Bet there is. Just about everyone has a bit of royalty in their background."

He chuckled. "You would know. Your Highness genealogist. Bet you can get me that information by next week."

Pippa's feeling of lightness sank. "Not next week now that Stefan is sending me on a trip," she said glumly.

"Where?"

"The place isn't the bad part. It's my escort."

Stefan's eyes widened. "Another escort?"

"Yes, that's what I said. I also told him I want to

ditch my security and move into an apartment away from the palace."

"Bet that went over well," Nic said in a dry tone.

She laughed. "Not at all. He ignored me."

Nic nodded. "You may have to go ahead and make your move before he has approved. And be prepared to be have your title taken away. Stefan is known for his priority on loyalty."

Her heart twisted at his words. He'd described Stefan perfectly. "I hate the idea of disappointing him. He's always counted on me not to cause any trouble."

"Sometimes you have to cause trouble if you're going to be who you're meant to be," Nic said.

His words vibrated through her. "When did you learn that?"

"When I was about eight years old," he said.

She smiled. "Wise words."

"Children are wiser more often than not. Where are you headed and when?"

"Capri, Italy, in three days. This is supposed to be a birthday gift, but I have to make two appearances and I have an escort who has a child as old as my youngest brother."

"Stefan's idea?" he said more than asked.

"Yes, they're trying to make a match. Bridget was trying to give me a hot, young sports guy. Stefan is always about the man who can bring added value to Chantaine. Ultimately, he was thrilled that Bridget fell for a doctor who became our medical director."

"But you have to live with the choices," Nic said.

She nodded. "I do."

"My mother will be crushed if we don't get a chance to celebrate your birthday," he said.

Pippa racked her brain for a time she could break away. "Friday afternoon."

"Night," he said.

She blinked at him. "Night?" she echoed. "How am I supposed to do that?" she asked.

"Creativity, ingenuity," he said. "You're a Devereaux," he said in a slightly mocking voice. "You can do it."

Pippa sighed. "I'll try to figure it out," she said. "I need to put on my disguise so I can return to the library."

"Unless you want to stay here," he said, his tone seductive.

Pippa wanted to stay far more than she should admit to anyone, including herself.

Nic told his mother about Pippa's birthday and she immediately asked Goldie to make a cake and instructed him to get ice cream and noise-making toys. At seven o'clock on Friday, Pippa arrived in a rush, wearing her horrid costume, and he'd never seen a more welcome sight. Greeting her at the gate, he helped her disassemble her disguise.

"You have no idea what I had to do to make this happen," she said, ripping off her wig and raking her fingers through her hair. She pulled a band from her wrist and pulled her hair up into a ponytail.

"We'll make it worth it," he said and led her toward the front door of the cottage. He knocked first.

She frowned at him. "Why are you knocking?" she asked.

"Don't discourage me. I'm being polite."

"Oh," she said, realization crossing over her face.

"Come in," a female voice called.

"Amelie is awake," she said.

Nic opened the door and Pippa walked inside.

"Surprise!" the small group cried. Streamers filled the air.

Pippa gaped. "Oh, my goodness." She clasped one of the streamers in her hand. She clearly couldn't help grinning. "How cool is this. You shouldn't have done it. I didn't expect it."

"We wanted to celebrate," Amelie said. "You deserved a party. Bring the cake, Goldie."

Seconds later, Goldie carried in a birthday cake with lit candles.

"Is that a fire hazard?" Nic joked.

Pippa frowned at him, then returned her gaze to the cake. "Oh, wow," she whispered.

Nic felt a ripple of pleasure at her obvious delight. "Ready to blow out those candles, Princess? Make a wish," he coached next to her ear.

"Just one?" she asked.

He chuckled. "As many wishes as you can fit in while you're putting out the candles."

"Okay," she said and bit her lip. She inhaled deeply and blew out the candles. Milliseconds after they were snuffed out, she looked at him and smiled. "I did it."

"So you did," he said.

"Time to cut the cake, eat the gelato, open gifts," Amelie said.

"Gifts," Pippa echoed. "There weren't supposed to be any gifts."

"Why not?" Amelie asked. "If there are birthday parties, there should be gifts."

Goldie served the cake and gelato, along with champagne. Mr. Lafitte then presented Pippa with a wrapped box.

"It's from me," Paul said.

"Really?" Pippa said and unwrapped the gift which held a box of chocolates and a bottle of champagne, along with a gift certificate to one of her favorite local shops.

"You did too much," she said, clearly surprised and delighted. "I didn't expect this."

"We Lafittes like the element of surprise. Don't forget that," he said with a broad wink.

"Thank you, Mr. Lafitte," she said and brushed a kiss over his cheek.

"Call me Paul, sweetheart," he said.

"Thank you, Paul," she said and another gift was given to her. She opened it to find a long knitted scarf.

Her eyes filled with tears, Pippa looked at Amelie. "Oh, no, you didn't."

"I fear I did," Amelie said with a laugh in her voice. "I realize it's not the best handiwork, but hopefully my effort will warm your heart."

"I will treasure it," Pippa said through a tight throat. She tried to remember when she'd had a birthday that had made her feel more special. She couldn't. For various reasons, her birthday had often been overlooked. There had been conflicting schedules. Her brothers and sisters had been busy. There were always more pressing obligations.

Tonight, however, she was the most important part of the Lafittes' evening. "I don't know what to say. You are—" Her voice broke and she swallowed hard over the lump of emotion lodging in her throat. "You have no idea how special this is for me."

"Bet you had gourmet cakes and birthday balls," Paul said.

"I had birthday cakes and birthday balls, but only a couple of times. My parents were rarely around for my birthdays. It was also sporadic for my brothers and sisters. Everyone was so busy," she said and shrugged, fearing she'd revealed too much. She bit her lip and smiled. "But this is fabulous. You've made me feel so special."

"That's because you *are* special," Amelie said and reached to embrace her.

Pippa hugged the woman and Amelie's gaunt frame frightened her. She was so thin. She felt so fragile. At the same time, Pippa had learned that Amelie was a strong, strong woman.

Goldie poured her another glass of champagne, but Pippa asked for water. She had to drive back to the palace.

"This has been delightful," Amelie said. "But I'm pooped. Tomorrow I'll be stronger, though, I promise," she said, wagging her finger.

"Of course you will," Pippa said. "I would expect nothing less. I have to go away for a few days, though, so I'll check in when I return."

Amelie frowned. "Away? We'll miss you."

"I'll miss you, too," Pippa said, hating the prospect of leaving the Lafittes behind. With Amelie in such fragile health, Pippa wondered if something would happen to her when she was gone on the Italian holiday.

"Good night, darling. Happy birthday," Amelie said. Paul followed, giving her a kiss on her cheek.

After they left, Pippa turned to Nic. "I should probably go."

"You didn't finish your cake," he said.

How could she? she wondered. She could barely breathe, let alone swallow Goldie's cake.

"You're gonna hurt Goldie's feelings," Nic added.

She winced. "I can't eat that entire cake," she whispered.

"Let's take part of it to the guest quarters. That should help," he said. "Bring your champagne."

She shook her head. "I have to drive back to the palace," she said.

"I'll handle that," he said.

"How?" she asked.

He shrugged. "Trust me."

Pippa decided, for once, to trust him. Heaven knew, she'd seen an entirely different side of him with the way he was dealing with his mother's illness. "Lead me on," she said, lifting her glass of champagne.

She followed him out the door and he led her into the guest bungalow. A breeze flowed through the window, more delicious than any central air-conditioning could ever be. "This feels nice in here. Have you had a hard time adjusting to the small quarters?"

"There are interruptions from my parents when I'm

working sometimes, but for the most part, I've liked it. I don't need that much space," he said.

She laughed. "I'm thinking of your yacht. It's huge."

"That's different," he said.

"And your ranch in Texas?" she asked. "Your big, big ranch? Is that different, too?"

"And your big, big palace?" he returned.

"I live in a small suite in the big, big palace," she said. "And I'm prepared to live in a small apartment."

"Why are you making the big move now?"

She shrugged and moved around the small den of the bungalow. "It's overdue. It just took me a while to see that."

"Have a seat," Nic said from behind her.

Too aware of his presence, she felt a dozen butterflies dancing in her stomach. She sank down onto the sofa and took a sip of her second glass of champagne. Nic sat beside her holding the plate with her piece of cake and soft gelato.

"It was better a few minutes ago," he said, scooping up a bite with a spoon and lifting it to her mouth.

She opened her mouth and swallowed the sweet treat. "It really is delicious. Goldie could be a bakery chef."

"Goldie is a lot of things," Nic said. "Bodyguard, medic, mechanic, cook. Hell, he would make a great nanny."

She smiled. "He's so big and brawny. That's a funny image." She took another bite of cake.

"All packed for your holiday?"

The cake stuck in her throat and she coughed. Nic handed her the glass of champagne. She took a quick sip, then shook her head. "No, I've procrastinated. The palace stylist chose some things for me, so I'll take them. I hate to admit it, but I'm dreading it, which is ridiculous. Who wouldn't be happy with a trip to Capri?" She made a face. "But with those appearances and the fact that I'm supposed to spend time with the count, it doesn't feel like a holiday. It feels like an assignment."

"Do you have any free time?"

"The last day," she said.

"I could meet you," he said.

Her heart stopped, then started at his suggestion. "Oh, that would be—" *Fantastic,* she thought before she stifled herself. "We shouldn't. I'm sure my bodyguard will be there."

He shrugged. "We could get around him," he said. "But if you'd rather not—"

"Are you sure you can leave Amelie?" she asked.

He nodded. "She's been fairly stable. It would be just a day or two. To be honest, I have business with a colleague in Rome. I've been putting it off. I could take care of business, then meet you in Capri."

Although she knew it was insanity to even consider a secret rendezvous, Pippa could not make herself say no. She opened her mouth to try to form the word and her lips refused. Her whole body and being wanted to be with Nic and she was bloody tired of denying herself. "Yes," she finally said and closed her eyes. "But this could be messy. You know that, don't you?"

Nic laughed. "I've been dealing with messes since I was six years old."

She wondered what it was about Nic that made her feel stronger. When she was with him, she felt as if she could do almost anything.

He met her gaze and he must have read her feelings in her eyes. Pulling her slowly toward him, he gave her a dozen chances to turn away, but she didn't. She couldn't. But she couldn't help wondering why he continued to pursue her. He was experienced. He could have any woman he wanted.

"Do you want me just because you can't have me?" she whispered, the fear squeezing out of her throat.

"No," he said. "Besides, we both know I can and will have you. The question is when," he said and lowered his mouth to hers.

Pippa melted into him. She was afraid to trust him, afraid to trust her feelings because she never really had before, but her fear of missing him was bigger than her fear of trusting him.

She kissed him back with all the passion in her heart and felt his surprise and pleasure ripple through her. He paused just a half beat before he kissed her more thoroughly.

She slid her fingers through his hair, craving the sensation of being as close to him as possible. He leaned back on the sofa and pulled her on top of him. She felt his arousal, swollen against her, and the knowledge made her even more crazy. She squeezed his shoulders and biceps and shuddered against him as he took her mouth in yet another kiss that took her upside down.

Pippa couldn't remember feeling this way. Even though she and Nic had been involved before, they'd never gone all the way. Now she wondered how she could possibly fight how much she wanted him.

She felt his hand tenderly rub her back. "Hey, you

know where this is headed, don't you?" he asked against her mouth.

Pippa moved her mouth from his and buried her head in his shoulder, taking desperate breaths.

"Pippa, are you sure you're ready?" he asked.

He wasn't going to make it easy for her. He was going to make her choose. And maybe that was part of the reason she wanted him so much. It was time.

She lifted her head to meet his gaze. "Yes, I am."

He sucked in a quick, sharp breath and chuckled. "I'm ready, too, but I want you to think about it a little longer."

Pippa blinked. "Pardon me, are you refusing to be with me?"

He rose to a sitting position with his arms still around her. "I don't want you to do something impulsive and regret it."

Anger flickered through her and she narrowed her eyes. "You sound like my family. You sound like you don't trust me to make my own decisions."

"It's not that. I'm protecting you," he said.

"That's what they say, too," she said. "No one trusts me to make my own decisions. No one," she said and pushed away from him.

"I'm going home," she said.

"I have to drive you," he said. "You've had too much champagne."

Pippa stood, wrapping her arms around her waist, feeling humiliated. "Goldie can take me."

*"I will take you,"* Nic said, rising.

Pippa bit her lip, feeling rejected and vulnerable. She wanted to hide.

"Pippa, you know I want you," he said and cupped her chin with his hand. "How much of a demonstration do you need?"

She swallowed over the desire pulsing through her. "It seems so easy for you to turn it off," she whispered.

He took her hand and placed it over his chest where his heart thundered against her palm. "Does that feel easy? I can show you more," he said as he moved her hand to his hard abdomen.

"S'okay," she said breathlessly.

"What do you want?" he asked.

"You've confused me," she said, clinging to him.

"Well, damn," he said. "Why would I do that?"

She looked up, studying his face. "I thought you would be the ruthless type when it comes to sex."

He held her against him for a long moment. "I am, but for some reason just not with you," he said.

Confusion and a half dozen other feelings swarmed through her like bees. The part of her that knew she was no beauty queen stabbed her with self-doubt. Pippa had made it a practice not to think about image, but all the criticism she'd received from the press over the years suddenly bombarded her. Maybe she wasn't sexy enough. Even though he'd been aroused, he'd been able to stop without a great deal of effort. At the same time, she'd lost all sense of time and place and could have gone much further without a second thought.

Self-conscious, she pulled away. "I really should get back to the palace," she said.

"Pippa—"

"I don't want to talk right now, if that's okay. I have

so much I need to do in a short amount of time to get ready for this trip."

With Goldie following in another vehicle, Nic drove her to the palace, and the silence between them was so uncomfortable that Pippa could barely stand it. Yes, she knew she'd told him she didn't want to talk, but now she would be leaving for her holiday, and she would just be full of doubts. Maybe it was for the best. Maybe this had been a close call and she could get her head back on straight with this trip.

He stopped a block away from the palace. "Can you make it the rest of the way?"

"Of course," she said. Overwhelmed by all the feelings tugging her in different directions, Pippa bit her lip. "Thank you for the birthday celebration and the ride to the palace. Listen, there's no need for you to make a special trip to Capri. I'll be there only a day and—"

"Are you saying you don't want me to come?" he asked, his gaze dark and penetrating.

She took a deep breath. "I'm saying you know my situation. I may not be able to spend time with you. The decision is completely up to you. *Ciao*," she said and got out of the passenger side of the car.

## Chapter Eight

Pippa arrived in Italy the next day. Count Bianchi greeted her at the airport. He was nearly bald with a paunch, but she tried very hard not to compare him to Nic. It was difficult because she had begun to compare every man to Nic.

"A pleasure to meet you, Your Highness," he said.

"And you, Count Bianchi," she said.

"Please call me Sal," he said. "You're such a lovely young woman. I'm pleased to have you by my side."

"Thank you very much, Sal," she said. "Tell me about your children."

During the ride, to Sal's chateau, she learned that Sal's oldest child was, in fact, older than her by five years. Sal also had several grandchildren. He showed her several photos and mentioned his wish to marry again.

Pippa rode the fence by praising his children but not

encouraging any discussion of her interest in him. After a quick respite in her room, she shared dinner with him in his formal dining room. Finally, they made the trip to the museum where Pippa made a brief speech encouraging historical and genealogical research.

Pippa begged off when Sal invited her to join him for a nightcap.

The following day, she geared up for a ride on a yacht, complete with photos. Afterward, she helped christen a new cruise ship with the count by her side. Every second, she damned Stefan for arranging this. Someone had clearly given the count entirely too much hope and she had to find a way to let him down easy. A chauffeur drove them back to his estate after the event.

"Have you enjoyed yourself?" the count asked, leaning toward her.

Pippa discreetly scooted away. "It's certainly been a long day. I'm more than ready for a good night of sleep."

"I understand you'll be in my country tomorrow night," the count said. "I would love to show you Capri. I know several restaurants and beaches that might please you."

"I couldn't trouble you," she said. "You've already done too much for me."

The count sighed.

"Sal, may I ask you? How long has it been since your wife passed away?" she asked.

He looked at her in surprise. "Ten months and three days."

She smiled and took his hand. "You're still counting days," she said gently. "I don't want to be presumptuous, but I don't think you're ready for a new wife. I know you're lonely, but I encourage you to take your time. You're a good man. You deserve a good woman."

He inhaled and smiled at her. "I'm an old fool to think I could attract a young princess like you."

She shook her head. "It's not that," she rushed to assure him. "I can tell that you're still not over your wife. I'm sorry for your pain, but at the same time, I know you're fortunate to have experienced that kind of love."

"Yes, I am," he said and began to talk about his former wife. Nearly an hour later, they arrived at his home. He appeared startled by the passage of time.

"I'm sorry if I've bored you," he said, clearly chagrined.

"No apologies necessary. I treasure a good love story, and that is what you and your wife had," she said.

"You're such a warm, lovely person. I wish I were at a different place in my mourning," he said.

"The right time will come," she said and pressed a kiss against his cheek. "The right woman will come."

He gave a soft chuckle. "Funny how the young can teach us so much," he said and helped her out of the limousine. "If I can ever do anything for you, it would be my pleasure," he said and kissed her hand.

"Thank you, Count Sal. My biggest wish for you is someone who will provide comfort to your heart. In the meantime, enjoy those grandchildren."

Sal gave a light laugh. "I'll take your advice."

The following morning, Pippa left the count's estate. After her last meeting with Nic, she wasn't sure he would meet her. She'd been so temperamental. He'd been so calm. His calmness infuriated her. She felt as if she couldn't control her passion. She didn't want to feel alone in her feelings and wanted to know that he felt the same way.

As she walked into her room with a lovely view of the ocean, Pippa stood in front of the open windows and inhaled the sea air. Her resort was located just outside the busy section of the beach, so she was able to enjoy the view without the crowds thronging to the pebbled beaches. Although Chantaine had its share of rocky beaches, Pippa had to confess Capri offered breathtaking vistas of steep cliffs, narrow gorges and limestone formations.

The sight was so beautiful she thought it might just clear her mind, and that was exactly what she needed. She refused to wonder if Nic would show or not. She had one day to truly relax and enjoy herself and that was what she intended to do. Pulling on the bathing suit the palace stylist had purchased for her, she glanced in the mirror and shrugged. Not too bad, she thought, then slathered herself with sunscreen from head to toe and grabbed her cover-up.

Situated on a hill, the hotel offered several decks with lounge chairs for sunning and enjoying the gorgeous views. Pippa accepted the assistance of staff to position an umbrella over her as she reclined in a chaise longue. She stared at the rocky coastline, willing it to clear her head. It occurred to her that Amelie would have loved this. The thought made her unbearably restless. Perhaps a magazine or book, she thought, rummaging through her bag. She pulled out the book on French history she'd been reading just before bedtime during the past month.

A shadow fell over her. Another waiter, she thought. Pippa had never been one to overindulge, especially when it wasn't even lunch yet. But perhaps a mimosa… She glanced up to see Nic standing over her.

Her heart lurched and the rush of pleasure she felt was so powerful that she couldn't squeak out a sound, let alone a word of greeting. He was dressed in jeans, a shirt and a ball cap, and his expression was gently mocking.

"Still pissed?" he asked.

She could argue that he was the basis for her *irritation* and confusion, but she was so bloody glad to see him that she knew it would be a waste. "Not too much."

"That's good. You want to chill here on the deck or are you in the mood for a little adventure?"

"Adventure," she said without waiting half a beat. "I'll tell my security I'm taking a tour."

Within a half hour, she was riding on the back of a motorcycle, clinging to Nic for her very life as he zigged and zagged around the curvy streets. If Stefan or Giles knew, they would have her head. Nic took another curve and she burst out laughing at the thrill.

"What's so funny?" he yelled at her.

"I'm terrified. I've either got to scream or laugh," she yelled back.

He nodded in approval. "We're just getting started."

After a lovely but terrifying ride, Nic pulled into the driveway of a chateau with stairs descending to a dock where several boats were moored. "What now?" she asked.

"We're going for another ride, this one on the ocean. You don't get seasick, do you?" he said, taking her hand.

She shook her head. "I'm a Devereaux. It's not allowed. My father never would have permitted it," she said as she walked down the steps with him.

"What trait would he have chosen over seasickness in his children?"

"Oh, I don't know. Two heads," she joked.

He stopped and looked at her and laughed. "You ought to get out more. I think it's good for you."

"And you?" she asked.

"Haven't had a lot of time for that lately," he said, his smile fading for a second. "But we've got today and a boat at our disposal."

"How did you arrange it?" she asked.

"My friend owns this chateau. He's out of town and he said I could use the house, the boat and the pool. I have access to a ski lodge in Switzerland he has used, so it all evens out." They walked across the dock and he helped her into a boat.

"Where are we going?" she asked.

He shot her a mysterious smile. "Places you can reach only by boat."

Joining him on the motorboat, Pippa reveled in the wind in her face. Nic didn't coddle her with a slow speed or by taking it easy on the curves. The wake made the ride bumpy enough that she had to sit down a few times.

"You're a fast pilot," she shouted to him. "Have you ever raced?"

He nodded. "But now we need to get to a special place."

"What special place?" she asked.

"You'll see soon enough," he said. He glanced over

his shoulder toward her. "Come here," he said extending his hand. "Wanna drive?"

Surprised by the offer, accepted his hand and he pulled her onto the seat next to him. "We have to slow down just a bit," she said.

He lowered the speed and she took the wheel. It was her first time because heaven knew her brother wouldn't have ever permitted it, let alone security. She gripped the steering wheel with her hands and turned it away from a huge yacht headed for the port side of their craft. The wake of the yacht created ripples, making the boat bounce against the waves.

Pippa laughed at the bumpiness but held tight.

"Doing good," Nic said, placing his hand at her back. It was a steadying sensation. Supportive, but not controlling. "Head this way," he said, pointing left.

She drove several more moments, then turned the wheel over to him. "Thank you. That was glorious," she said, unable to wipe her smile from her face.

"Glad you enjoyed it," he said, then revved up the speed again. "Hold on, Your Highness."

After several minutes, Nic slowed as they drew close to a series of rocks jutting from the ocean. "Where are we going?"

"Guess," he said, slowing the speed even more.

In the distance, she saw a rowing boat. Realization hit her. "The Blue Grotto," she said, so excited she could hardly stand it. "I know it's supposed to be a huge tourist spot, but I've always wanted to see it."

"I was hoping," he said.

"But it's supposed to be incredibly crowded." She glanced at Nic. "Why is it deserted? Is there a problem?"

"I bought an hour for us. No other boats during that time," he said.

She blinked. "That would be obscenely expensive," she said. "Stefan would throw a fit if he knew."

"He doesn't have to know," Nic said with a smile. He pulled closer to the rowboat and dropped anchor. The guide from the rowboat pulled right up next to their motorboat. Nic and the guide assisted her onto the rowboat.

*"Buongiorno,"* the man said. "I'm Roberto. I will be your guide."

*"Buongiorno* and *grazie,* Roberto. I'm very excited to see the Blue Grotto," she said.

Nic hopped aboard. "Just tell me you've got a great singing voice," he said and shook Roberto's hand.

Roberto's mouth lifted in a wide grin. "The best. When I tell you, you must lie down in the boat." He turned to Nic. "Hold on to your sweetheart."

Pippa sank to a sitting position. Nic sat behind her and wrapped his arms around her. "Just following orders," he said.

She laughed, feeling the same terror and exultation she'd felt on the motorcycle and the speedboat. As they drew closer to the famous cave, she and Nic reclined in the boat.

"Prepare to enter the Blue Grotto, a spectacle providing thrills since the Roman times. Statues of pagan gods rest on the floor of the grotto. Once inside, you will see a surreal view that will make you feel as if you are floating through a clear sky. The reflection of the sunlight produces a unique transparency. There is no bluer blue," Roberto said. "Stay low, then you may sit up for a few minutes."

Sitting cradled in Nic's arms, Pippa stared in wonder at the blue universe on which they floated. They could have been riding on the sky if not for the lapping sound of the ocean against the cave walls.

"Put your hands in the water," Roberto said.

Both Nic and Pippa dipped their fingers into the cool water.

"It's so beautiful," she said.

"As are you, *signorina*," he said, and began to sing *"Bella Notte."* The acoustics were amazing. She almost didn't want to breathe because she didn't want to miss a nuance of the experience. Surrounded by Nic's strength and the wonder of the Blue Grotto, Pippa wanted to absorb everything. This was the kind of magic she wanted to store up inside her for sad, bad days.

When Roberto sang the last note, she glanced up at Nic. "This was amazing," she said.

"Quite a show," he said and took her mouth in a kiss.

After they boarded the motorboat, Nic took them back to the chateau. "Are you starving?" he asked. "My friend offered me anything in his pantry and refrigerator, but I thought we'd order takeout. The view is great and I thought you'd just as soon skip a public restaurant."

"That sounds perfect," she said and joined him as they climbed the steps to the chateau. Chugging her water, she sank onto a chair on the patio which overlooked the sea and sighed in contentment as she heard Nic call in an order to a restaurant.

Nic sat down across from her, lifting a bottle of beer to his lips. "You like Capri?"

"How could I not?" she said and shook her head. "I've never had a day like this."

"It was pretty good, wasn't it?"

"That's an understatement, and you know it," she said.

He chuckled at her response.

"Perhaps you do these kinds of things on a far more regular basis," she said.

"I've had some thrills, but the person you share it with can make a big difference," he said. "You need to make any calls to your security guy?"

She made a face at the reminder. "He said for me to call him when I returned to my room." She drummed her fingers on the table. "I suppose I could tell him I've returned and I'm safe and sound."

"Your choice," he said and took another drink from his beer.

Her stomach dancing with a combination of anticipation and apprehension, she placed the call. Her security man seemed satisfied. "I'd like to freshen up," she said and Nic pointed her to the toilet.

When she looked in the mirror, she nearly didn't recognize herself. Her cheeks and lips were flushed a deep pink. Her eyes looked so blue against the contrast of her skin and her hair was wilder than she'd ever seen it. Pippa chuckled and shook her head. It was hopeless. There was no use trying to tame it.

Dinner arrived and she and Nic enjoyed a meal of pasta, seafood and wine. Pippa knew Nic joked to diffuse tensions and cover his feelings, but she knew underneath it all, he had his share of stress. She'd never seen him this relaxed since she'd met him.

"You enjoy the sea. It's therapeutic for you," she said, touching his arm.

"It can be. It's not always." He shrugged. "What about you? Do you enjoy boating?"

She shrugged. "I haven't always. When I was a child, my father was known for spending as much time on his yacht as possible. He missed birthdays, appointments so he could escape on his yacht. In retrospect, he must not have been a very happy man."

"Tough being crown prince," Nic said with a wry grin.

"Perhaps. Some are better suited for the job than others. Stefan takes it very seriously, sometimes too seriously in my opinion. He's very controlling. I remember once when I was a teenager, we were on a family outing on the yacht and I asked if I could take the wheel just for a moment."

"Let me guess," Nic said. "He refused. There are plenty of men who can't give up the wheel."

"Why did you let me?" she asked. "For all you knew, I could have wrecked the boat."

"You're excessively responsible, Pippa. If you'd been concerned, you would have asked for my help. Plus, you underrate your abilities," he said in a matter-of-fact voice as he took another sip of red wine.

"You can't know that. I could be a total klutz," she said. "For all you know, we could be in a hospital from my flipping that boat."

He shot her a sideways glance full of humor. "I have excellent instincts."

She sighed and took a sip of her own wine. "Well, I can't argue with that."

"Anything else you want to argue about?" he asked, swirling his wine in his glass.

She couldn't help chuckling. She had been a bit contrary. "No."

"Good," he said. "Want to go for a swim in the pool? We can turn out the lights."

Pippa was still wearing her swimsuit under her clothes. The invitation for an evening swim was irresistible. She stood. "I'm ready."

He chuckled at her immediate reaction. "I should have asked earlier. I'll grab some towels. Let's go."

Cutting the lights, Nic grabbed some towels and led her down to the pool with a flashlight. Pippa tripped on a step, but he caught her against him. "Okay?" he asked.

"Yes. It's so dark," she said, laughing nervously.

"That's the idea," Nic said and led her the rest of the way to the pool. Clouds cast a filmy cover over the moon, but there was some light reflected against the water of the pool.

"It's beautiful," she said.

Nic jumped into the pool, the splash spraying over her legs. "It is," he said, with a wicked smile on his gorgeous wet face. "Come on in."

She paused half a second and jumped in. Two seconds later, she felt Nic's arms around her. "It's a little chilly."

"You'll warm up in a minute. Trust me," he said, pulling her against him.

She looked up into his face, feeling a crazy joy at the sight of the droplets on his face. "You're not warm," she said. "You're hot."

"I'm that way every time I get around you," he said and dipped his mouth to hers for a quick kiss.

The brief touch of his mouth on hers made her sizzle and burn deep inside.

She instinctively wrapped her legs around his waist.

"I like that," he said, pressing his hand at the back of her waist.

Everything that had been brewing between them for months tightened so much that she could hardly breathe. "Whew," she breathed.

"Take it easy," he said. "You okay?"

"Yeah," she breathed.

"You look like you need another kiss," he said with a half grin and lowered his mouth.

She sank into his mouth, feeling him, inhaling him. She couldn't get enough. His tongue slid past her lips and she savored the taste of him, the feel of him wrapped around her. The buoyancy of the water only added to the sensuality of the experience.

Nic slid his hands over her thighs and cupped her hips as he gave her a French kiss that made her feel as if she were turning upside down. She felt the same excitement race through her that she'd experienced earlier today when she'd driven the boat.

He squeezed her against himself. "I love your laugh," he muttered against her mouth.

"Good thing," she said. "I can't remember laughing more than I do with you."

"Hold your breath." He kissed her again, twirled her around again and sank, inch by inch underwater. It was a crazy, sexy, amazing experience kissing Nic that way. Seconds later, he rose, bringing her to the surface. She sucked in a quick breath of air, staring into his face. His strong, sexy face was covered with droplets of water. His eyes bored into hers.

The electricity between them sizzled and burned. She lifted her hands to cradle his face. "You're quite an amazing man."

He stopped dead. "That's quite the compliment," he said.

"I'm just telling the truth," she said.

"Good to know," he said and untied the top of her bathing suit. His hands slid over her breasts.

She inhaled quickly.

"You want me to stop?" he asked.

She hesitated a half beat. "No," she whispered.

He leaned his forehead against hers. "Pippa, I'm not gonna wanna stop," he said.

Her heart slamming against her ribs, she bit her lip. "Neither am I."

They played and frolicked in the pool. He kissed and caressed her, coaxing her out of the bottom of her bathing suit so that she swam nude with him. They got each other so worked up that he almost took her in the pool. Instead, he dragged her from the pool, wrapped a towel around her, another around him and half carried her up the stairs to the house.

Carrying her to the master bed and following her down, he seemed to devour her. And Pippa wanted him to consume her.

"Are you sure you're okay with this?" he asked, clearly reining himself under control.

"Yes," she said and stretched her arms out to him.

Nic slid his hand between her thighs, testing her

readiness. He rubbed and caressed her, making her wet with wanting. Sliding his finger inside her, he drove her even further. He made her want deep inside her.

"Nic," she said, squeezing his arms.

"You want me?" he asked, his voice raspy with his own desire.

"Yes," she said, close to pleading.

He slid his lips down to her breast, taking one of her nipples in his mouth. The sensation electrified her. She felt the instant connection between her breast and lower, deeper inside her.

"I want you inside me," she said. "In me."

In some corner of her mind, she knew he was putting on protection. Seconds later, he pushed her thighs apart. He thrust inside her and she felt a rush of shock and burning pain at the invasion. "Oh," she said.

Nic stopped, staring at her in surprise. He swore under his breath. "You should have told me."

"I wasn't thinking about it," she said. "My mind was on—" She wiggled as she grew more accustomed to him. "Being with you," she said and wiggled again.

His gaze darkened and he fastened his hands around her hips. "You're gonna make this tough on me," he said in a rough voice.

"Hopefully, it won't be all bad."

Nic groaned and began to move in a slow, delicious rhythm. Pippa felt the beginning of exquisite sensations sliding throughout her.

"You okay?" he asked in a low, uneven voice.

"Yesssss," she said. "This is sooo—" The twist of tension growing inside her took her breath.

The pulsing rhythm continued, and she clung to him,

staring into his dark gaze, taking and feeling taken. His jaw tightened with restraint, he reached down between her legs and sought her sweet spot, sending electrical impulses through her. The combination of his possession and his caresses were too much.

She jerked and rippled in response. Suddenly, her body clenched in indescribable pleasure and she arched toward him. "Nic," she called, feeling as if her voice were separated from her body.

He held her tight and she felt and heard his own climax ripple through her.

It was the most profound experience of her life and she knew she would never, ever be the same.

Their harsh breaths mingled in the air. The sound was as primitive as what she'd just experienced. At this moment, she felt Nic inside her body, her mind, her blood. She wondered if she would ever breathe without being aware of him again.

## Chapter Nine

Nic lay on his side and pulled Pippa against him. She was half asleep. He tried to take in the impact of what they'd done. Nic had known it was inevitable. He had known they would make love. He had known she would be his.

He just hadn't known how much it would affect him. Months ago, when he'd first met Pippa, he'd wanted her, reluctantly felt a need for her. Something primal had driven him toward her. He'd hoped it had all been about sex, but now he knew he'd been wrong.

Something in his psyche was tangled with this woman, and he wasn't sure how in hell he could untangle himself from her. Aside from the fact that she felt so soft and right nestled against him, he felt himself wanting more. Wanting something he hadn't known was possible.

It didn't make sense. Other women had made themselves available to him. Sometimes he'd accepted their overtures. Sometimes he'd refused. Now, he felt himself falling deeper than he'd ever expected.

He frowned as he luxuriated in her naked body against his. He'd thought that once he took her, he would be okay. He would be rid of the itch that plagued him day and night for her. But it hadn't worked. Now that he'd taken her, it was almost as if he was more committed. He wanted her more.

That was strange as hell.

He slid his hand over her crazy, curly hair. She sighed and the sound did something crazy to his gut. He felt incredibly protective of her. More so now. He knew she was mostly asleep, but her hand closed over his, as if she were protecting him. The notion was amusing, but the gesture stole his heart.

The rude ping of his cell phone awakened Nic. It took a few pings, but he finally recognized the sound. Grabbing his cell phone from the bedside table, he pulled it up to his ear. "Yes," he said.

"Nic," his father said. "Your mother's in trouble. She needs help. The regular doctor can't be reached."

Nic sat up straight in bed. "What's wrong?"

"Her belly's distended. She's in pain," his father said.

"I'll take care of it," Nic said. "I'll be there soon."

Pippa opened her gloriously blue, groggy eyes. "What's wrong?"

"Amelie is having problems. Her belly's distended."

Pippa frowned, rising in the bed. "Oh, no. Your doctor isn't available?"

Nic scowled. "He should have been. She may need

to have some sort of draining from fluid buildup. I may have to find another doctor."

Pippa blinked, then frowned again. "If it takes too long, maybe I can find another doctor."

"Who?" he asked.

"My brother-in-law, Ryder McCall," she said.

"Won't that cause problems for you?" he asked.

"What's more important?" she asked. "My problems, or your mother's?"

Two hours later, they were on a plane, in different rows, to Chantaine. Even though she wasn't sitting next to him, Pippa could feel Nic's tension reverberating throughout the jet. She wished she could help him, but ultimately, she knew she couldn't. Ultimately, she knew Amelie would die. And she would die soon. The question was how could they make Amelie's passing easy. The jet landed in Chantaine and she exited the plane ahead of Nic.

Needing to get away from the watchful eye of Giles, her security man, she made a quick trip to the ladies' room.

Nic called her on her cell. "I can take her to a clinic, but that won't guarantee her privacy. The news could get out that she's here."

"Wait," she said. "Let me see what I can do."

She took several deep breaths, then dialed the number for her brother-in-law, Ryder. He immediately answered.

"Ryder McCall," he said.

"This is Pippa," she said. "Don't reveal who you're speaking to. It's an emergency."

He paused a half beat. "How can I help you?"

"There's a cancer patient who needs some kind of draining. I'm hoping you can help."

He paused again. "Where can I meet you?"

Pippa gave him the address. An hour later, she arrived at the cottage and met with Nic. "Ryder is coming."

"Can he help?" he asked as they stood in the den. Amelie was in the bedroom, bloated and suffering.

Paul banged his crutch on the floor. "She's in pain. What's taking so damn long?" he demanded.

"Ryder will be here any moment," Pippa tried to reassure him.

"Ryder?" Paul echoed. "Who the hell is Ryder? What kind of doctor is named Ryder?"

Seconds later, Pippa's brother-in-law strode into the house. He met Pippa's gaze. "How sick is she?" he asked.

"She's terminal," she said in a low voice. "We want to keep her as comfortable as possible," she said.

Ryder met her gaze. "You should share this with your family," he said.

"My family wouldn't understand," she said. "You know how much they hate the Lafittes."

"I don't understand the grudge," Ryder muttered.

"I need your help and your confidence," she said.

"The first is easy. The second is not. Soon, you must tell your family about this," he said.

Pippa felt her stomach twist. "There's enough trouble today," she said. "Please help Amelie."

Moments later, Goldie drove Amelie to a local clinic

where Ryder performed the procedure that would bring her relief.

Just a few hours passed and Amelie was brought home.

"Thank you," Nic said, clearly weary from the whole experience. "How much trouble will this cause you?"

Pippa shrugged. "Ryder will give me some time. It's more important that Amelie is okay."

Nic's gaze grew shuttered. "You know it's only a matter of time for her," he said.

"I know that," she said. "But I want her to be as comfortable as possible."

He took her hand and clasped it for a long moment. "How did I get so damn lucky to know you?"

She smiled. "That's an excellent question. I feel the same way about you."

In the middle of the night, Pippa returned to the palace. Happily enough, she didn't have to endure a screening from her security detail. Unfortunately that didn't extend to Bridget. Her sister could out-snoop any P.I., and Pippa was doomed to face her questions.

"How was the count? Was he a prick? Was he determined to get into your pants?" she asked as Pippa gulped down her first coffee of the day.

"He was lovely. Just older. We both realized that he was still in love with his wife and he should take his time before getting involved with anyone else even though he was lonely."

Bridget blinked. "Really?"

Pippa nodded. "Really."

"So what did you do for the rest of your trip in Capri?"

"I took a tour," Pippa said.

"A tour?" Bridget echoed, chagrined. "The least the count could have done was to give you a proper tour of Capri."

"I didn't want him to do it," Pippa said. "He was a sweet man, but I used up all my patience during the two days I spent with him. I just needed to take a break after that."

"I suppose I can understand that. I feel bad that you've experienced such bad matchups from Stefan and me," Bridget said.

"There are worse things," Pippa said.

"True," Bridget said. "Ryder went out last night to help a terminal cancer patient."

Pippa's stomach clenched. "How terrible."

Bridget shook her head. "He has a difficult job."

Pippa nodded. "Yes, he does," she murmured.

Bridget shrugged. "Well, did you enjoy Capri? I hate to think the whole trip was a waste."

Pippa nodded again. "Yes, I got to see the Blue Grotto. It was amazing."

"Did you really take a tour?" Bridget asked.

"Yes," Pippa said. "The sight of it was amazing. Worth the crowd."

Bridget shook her head. "Better you than me. I would love to see it, but I couldn't stand the crowds."

"It wasn't that crowded when I was there," Pippa said. "I guess I got lucky."

"Did the guides sing for you?" Bridget asked.

"'*Bella Notte,*'" she said with a smile.

"How romantic," Bridget said. "A shame you didn't have a handsome man accompanying you."

"It was beautiful," Pippa said.

Bridget sighed. "You're a saint. You know how to make the best of everything."

"I would never call myself a saint," Pippa said.

"That's because you don't know what demons the rest of us are," Bridget said with a dirty giggle.

"You overstate your evil," Pippa said. "Most of us just do the best we can."

"That attitude is what makes you a saint," Bridget told her.

Guilt stabbing at her. She was lying to her family. "Please don't call me a saint. I'm not worthy of that," Pippa said.

Bridget tilted her head, studying Pippa's face. "If you insist," she said. "But if anyone ever deserved saint-hood—"

"It wouldn't be me," Pippa said in a flat voice.

Stefan wouldn't meet with her the following day. His assistant said he was too busy. After soldiering through her brother's romantic aspirations for her with the count, Pippa was more than peeved, so she took a rare move. She sent him an email and text. In general, the family was instructed not to bother Stefan with personal texts. She usually respected the instruction. After all, she knew he had a terribly demanding schedule and she didn't want to add to his burden. Today, her patience wore thin.

Happy birthday to me. I'm moving out and ditching my security. Cheers, Pippa.

Seconds later, she received a text from Stefan. I order you not to make any changes before you and I have an opportunity to talk.

She sent a return text. Apologies. You used up your orders when you tried to match me up with a man nearly the age of our father. *Ciao*.

Then she turned off her phone. Pippa felt a rush of adrenaline race through her. Her heart hammered against her rib cage. She was so rarely defiant. She exulted in the feeling. For a moment. Then she realized she needed to find a place to live. Immediately.

She spent the morning making calls to apartments, eliminating those without a security gate. By afternoon, she had a list of properties and made visits. At five-thirty, she signed a lease for a one-bedroom apartment. It cost a little more than she'd hoped, but the situation was perfect for her. Now if she could just ditch her security detail.

Pippa finally turned on her phone again, dreading the incoming voice mails and messages. She was immediately deluged by messages from Stefan, some of which had been written in all capital letters. She deleted them without reading and sent one last message regarding her security and the fact that she was ready to make a press release regarding her status change in security.

A half beat later, her phone rang, and her stomach immediately tightened. Pippa saw that it was Stefan and considered pushing the ignore button. *Coward.* Scowling at the truth in the accusation, she picked up the call. "Good evening, Your Royal Highness," she said.

"What in bloody hell has gotten into you?" Stefan demanded. "I realize getting you together with the count was a stretch, but your overreaction is totally unnecessary."

"It's not an overreaction. I just turned twenty-five," she said.

"But you've never complained before," Stefan said. "I can't allow you to move out and dismiss your security. Are you sure you're not having some sort of women's issue?"

If his pompous attitude weren't so offensive, she would have laughed. "Pretend I'm male and this will all seem overdue," she said.

"But you're not. You're my youngest sister and it's my duty to protect you."

Her heart softened. "That's so sweet, Stefan, and I do appreciate it, but I will die of suffocation if I stay at the palace. It's time for me to go."

"I don't understand this. You've always been so reasonable," he said.

"Acquiescent," she corrected. "I feel like Rapunzel, but with bad hair."

Stefan sighed. "At least continue your security."

"No. My security is a leash. It's unnecessary except when I make appearances assigned by the palace. Trust me, the citizens of Chantaine will cheer when they see another expense deducted by the palace."

"They won't know about it until after the fact," Stefan said and swore. "Promise you'll still attend family dinners," he added.

"I will," she said, her heart softening again. "You're so busy you won't notice that I'm gone."

"I already notice," he said.

Pippa felt her eyes burn with tears. Her emotions

caught her off guard, but she refused to give in to them. "I promise to babysit your new child," she said. "None of the new generation of Devereauxs will escape my terrible singing voice."

Stefan laughed. "I love you, Pippa."

Pippa's heart caught. For her hardnosed brother to admit such feelings aloud was monumental. It was all she could do to choke the words through her throat. "And I love you."

They hung up, and Pippa began to weep.

The following day, she enlisted the help of security to help her move into her apartment. She was able to make her move under the radar of Bridget because her sister was busy with the construction of the new so-called ranch. Pippa didn't want her security man to get a hernia, so she insisted he get help.

By noon, she was moved into her apartment. Surprisingly enough, she had more room in her new quarters than her previous suite at the palace. She felt a strange combination of relief and anxiety.

Sinking down onto the antique sofa that seemed so out of place in her new surroundings, she took a deep breath. She was free. That was what she'd wanted. Right?

A knock on the door startled her. She rose, looked through the peephole and saw Nic standing outside her door. She whipped the door open. "How did you find me? And how did you get through security?"

"Goldie," he said with a shrug. "You gonna invite me in?"

Fighting a sudden, strange awkwardness, she nodded. "Of course."

He stepped inside and glanced around. "Downsizing?" he asked.

"Actually the apartment is larger than my quarters at the palace," she said, folding her arms over her chest.

"Really," he said more than asked as he glanced around the apartment. "Did they put you in the palace dungeon or something?"

She laughed. "No, but I had no children, so I didn't need a larger suite. How did Goldie find out about my move?"

Nic shrugged. "Goldie has his ways. I don't question him. He just gets the job done. Why didn't you tell me about your plans for the big move?"

"Besides the fact that I didn't know if it would all work out, I don't owe anyone an explanation about my plans," she said.

He gave a low whistle and dipped his head. "As you say, Your Highness."

She wrinkled her nose at his response. "Truthfully, would you feel the need to make explanations about your own living arrangements?"

He met her gaze and gave another shrug. "Touché. I'm just curious what inspired all this."

"It's been a long time coming," she said, walking toward the balcony window. "Stefan fought it every inch of the way. I know he means well, but it will take him a long time to understand what I said about feeling like Rapunzel with very bad hair."

"I like your hair," Nic said.

She laughed, her heart warming at his comment. "That's not the point. I must confess I'm a bit worried that it was so easy for Goldie to find me. If he can get through the security, others could, too."

"Not likely," Nic said. "Many foreign nations could learn a lot from Goldie."

"But how did you get through?" she asked.

"I'm interested in buying the entire complex," he said.

Pippa blinked. "Pardon me?"

"It's just a story, but you never know," he said. "Have you ordered pizza?"

"What do you mean?"

"It's a tradition. Whenever you move, you order pizza for dinner because you're too tired for anything else," he said.

"I hadn't thought of it, but—"

"It's on me," he said with a sexy smile. "Because I didn't get here fast enough to help you move in."

Her heart softened. "That's very nice," she said.

"I have ulterior motives," he confessed. "I want you to share it with me."

"I can do that," she said.

Forty-five minutes later they sat with their feet propped on the boxes, munching on a loaded pizza. "I would have chosen vegetarian," Pippa said, but took a bite of her second slice anyway.

Nic shook his head. "No. Moving day turns everyone into a carnivore."

"If you say so," she said, smiling at him. "What made you put Goldie on me?"

"When I didn't hear from you, I got worried. I didn't know how hard your family would be on you once they learned about your relationship with the Lafittes."

"They still don't know," she said, taking a long draw from her glass of water.

He shot her a look of disbelief. "You sure?"

"Reasonably sure. I can't believe neither Stefan nor Bridget would be able to hold back their opinions if they knew. They're both extremely outspoken," she said.

"Bet Stefan hated that you moved out. I don't think he thought you would go through with it," he said.

"Hate is a mild term for it," she said, smiling at him. "And you're right. He didn't believe I would go through with it even though I'd warned him."

He grinned at her in return. "I'm surprised the palace didn't disintegrate from his temper tantrum."

"The palace has endured temper tantrums over the course of several centuries," she said. "I must confess I wonder if Stefan has cracked a few walls."

"Well, he's turning the tide. He's no playboy prince," Nic said. "That kind of will is going to shake some foundations."

Pippa nodded. "That's a good way of saying it. Stefan has fought to overcome my father's reputation."

"I'd say he's doing a pretty damn good job."

"He is. I've tried to support him, but I had to move away from the palace. I couldn't stand the restraints anymore."

"The timing's interesting. Did the Lafittes have anything to do with your decision?"

"Perhaps," she said. "You're all such independent sorts, even Amelie. You made me aware of how trapped I feel."

"And how do you feel now?" he asked.

"Great," she said, reluctant to reveal even her tiniest regret.

"And a little scared," he said.

"I didn't say that," she said.

"Your mouth didn't, but your eyes did," he said and cupped her chin. "You're gonna be okay, Pippa. You're stronger than anyone thinks."

"What makes you so sure?" she asked.

He gave a dry chuckle. "You've already proven yourself ten times over."

The strength in his gaze both empowered and aroused her. The combination of feelings was strange but undeniable. She leaned toward him and he took her mouth. The room began to spin.

The kiss turned into another and another. Soon enough, he'd removed her blouse and skirt. She pushed away his shirt and jeans, and he was inside her. This time, slowly.

"Okay?" he asked, his restraint vibrating from his body.

"Yes," she said, drawing him into her.

The rhythm began. She took him and he filled her. More than ever, they had more in common. She was a rebel just like him, and their joining was more powerful with the knowledge of it.

The next morning, Nic awakened before dawn on the mattress on which they'd collapsed on the floor. Pippa breathed in a deep, even sleep. She'd been exhausted and he could still feel her tiredness against him. But Nic had tasks calling him, even at this time of day. His businesses, his father's business, his mother's illness.

He tried to make himself slow down and relax for just a few moments.

"You're awake," Pippa whispered and turned her face into his throat.

His heart stuttered. "How did you know?"

"Your whole body is tense. I can almost feel your mind clicking a million kilometers an hour," she said.

He felt the slightest easing inside him. "I thought you were asleep."

She gave a soft chuckle that tickled his throat. "Not."

He tugged her fabulous, curly hair with one hand and slid his hand low between her legs. "As long as you're awake."

She gave a soft intake of breath. "Oh, my."

"Oh, yeah," he said and began to make love to her.

An hour later, they took a shower together and had to hunt for towels. They dried off with blankets instead which provided even more of a distraction.

Nic dressed in the clothes he'd worn the day before. Pippa stood before him with a damp blanket wrapped around her.

"Will you be okay?" he asked.

"Of course," she said. "I have a dozen boxes to unpack. My biggest fear of the day is a visit from Bridget or a call from Tina."

He rubbed her shoulders. "You can handle them."

"Yes, it just won't be fun," she said and made a face.

"Call me if you need me to break any legs," he said.

She laughed. "Now that would go over well."

"I'll check in on you later, but seriously, call me if you need me," he said.

"I will," she said. "And I may take a break from unpacking to visit your mother."

"She would like that," he said. "She did okay physically after the procedure to drain extra fluid, but I can tell it bothered her to need it."

She sighed. "I wish I could change this for her."

"You already have," he said.

"Have you been able to reach your brothers?" she asked.

"Two down, one to go," he said. "They said no the first three times I talked to them. I've got them up to a maybe."

"You're amazing and they're stupid," she said.

"It's complicated with my dad," he said. "If I hadn't been successful on my own so young, I may have shared their attitude. The weird thing about that success is that it freed me to forgive him."

Pippa loved him even more for his ability to express how he'd grown. Not every man could do that. She reached for his hand. "You're a good man."

His hand enclosed hers. "Careful. Never forget that I come from pirates."

## Chapter Ten

Nic chewed through another two antacids as he stared at his electronic tablet and tried to figure out when he could break away for a two-day business trip. His mother had seemed more tired than usual lately, sleeping more during the day. He didn't know what in hell to do. If he left and she passed, he would never forgive himself.

He had thought that spending the day and night with Pippa in Capri would rid him of the increasing edginess he'd felt 24/7. Being with Pippa calmed a part of him, and he'd thought just a little time away with her would give him the break he'd never admit to needing.

He'd known going into this that it would be no picnic, but he would never have predicted the effect the situation would have on his body. He had begun to feel like a caged animal, rarely sleeping longer than three hours at night. The knowledge of his mother's impending death seemed to squeeze his throat tighter and tighter every day. He was always running out of antacids. He'd been determined to keep his emotions under strict control, but his frustration at his inability to change his mother's pain and the ugly progress of her disease wore him down.

He heard the sound of his mother singing outside his window and immediately glanced outside. He stared in disbelief at the sight of her as she approached the pool. It was 1:00 a.m.

Alarmed, Nic raced out the door. "Mother, what in hell are you doing?"

Amelie glanced over her shoulder. "Oh, hello, darling. What are you doing up so late?"

Nic felt a sliver of relief. At least she was lucid. He let out a half breath. "Finishing up some work," he said, moving toward her. Although she was still eating, she looked thinner.

Amelie tilted her head, sympathy creasing her brows. "You're not sleeping well, are you?" she said more than asked. "Come here and sit with me for a few minutes. I was going to go for a swim, but it can wait," she said as she sank into a chair.

Nic shook his head, but joined her. "You can't go swimming. Dr. McCall said you have to wait for five days after the procedure to swim or take a tub bath."

She frowned. "I could have sworn it's already been five days." She waved her hand. "My memory's not the best lately. The pain meds help the pain, but they make me sleepy. Makes for a difficult choice." She sighed. "But enough about me. I'm sick of it all being about me. How are you and Pippa?"

"What do you mean me and Pippa?" he asked, rubbing his jaw.

"Well, there's obviously something between you. It's a wonder the sparks don't burn down the cottage. What are you going to do about it?"

"It's complicated," he said.

She laughed. "You think I don't understand complications?"

"She's very devoted to her family. They hate me. It's an impossible situation for her. I can't ask her to give up her family," he said.

"Pippa is a very strong woman. You're a strong man. The two of you together, you may be able to achieve something that seems impossible," she said.

Nic couldn't see it. He couldn't see asking such a thing of Pippa after all she'd already done for him and his mother.

"You have no faith," she said. "You'll have to find your way. But remember what I said."

"I will," he said.

"And I wish you wouldn't suffer so much about the fact that I'm dying. I'm going to be fine. I'm a bit worried about your father, but I think if you get him a dog, it will help."

Nic blinked. "A dog?"

His mother nodded. "He'll need the blind adoration and companionship. Trust me on this."

His stomach knotted at the direction of their conversation. "We don't have to talk about this."

"Yes, we do," she said and put her hand over his. "I'm worried about you."

He clenched his jaw. "You don't need to worry about me. You raised me to be strong."

"Yes, but you don't have superpowers. Deep inside, you think you should be able to save me, and the fact that you can't is ripping you apart. If I'd known it would be this hard for you, I would have stayed in the States and worked with hospice. This has been too much of a burden on you."

"I wouldn't have it any other way," he said. "Except for you not to die," he said, his eyes stinging with emotion.

"Oh, darling, you will always have me with you," she said. "I promise. And I believe you'll feel it. It will hurt terribly in the beginning, but I'll always be with you. You're doomed. You have my genetic material and that won't go away."

He laughed at her words, struggling with a dozen emotions, most of them sad and wrenching. "Is there anything else I can do for you?"

"You've already done it. You've given me this wonderful gift of time in Chantaine. Now live your life," she said. "If you need to take care of business, do it. But don't forget your heart. Never ever forget to have fun and to have heart. Promise?" she asked.

He took a deep breath. "I promise."

She looked wistfully at the pool. "Are you sure you won't let me cheat and take a quick dip?"

"One more day, and you can be a dolphin. But not until."

"You're such a tyrant," Amelie said. "But I'm tired again anyway. Good night, darling. Try to get some rest. You know how cranky you get when you don't get your beauty sleep."

He rolled his eyes. "I'll try," he said and helped her to her feet and walked her to the front door. At that moment, he knew what he had to do. She hadn't asked for it, but there was one more thing his mother wanted and he was damn well going to do it for her.

The next day, Pippa came to visit. She began pulling off her disguise the second she climbed out of the car. "Hate this," she muttered. "Completely and totally hate this."

Even her griping made Nic feel a little lighter. He stepped outside his door and grabbed her from behind. She gave a squeal.

"It's me," he assured. "The gray wig brings out my primal urges," he said.

She laughed breathlessly and turned toward him. "You're insane."

"I do my best," he said. "It's damn good to see you." He took her mouth in a long kiss that made him want far more than a kiss.

"I've been unpacking," she said. "I didn't think I had that much, but I clearly underestimated. Plus, I had nothing in my refrigerator and couldn't ring the chef for breakfast or dinner."

"Oooh, tough break, Your Highness. Sure you don't want to move back into the palace?" he asked. "I know Stefan would take you back."

She shook her head. "There will be adjustments. That's expected. Nothing a toaster and microwave won't cure. Plus I'm told my security detail is retiring at the end of this week. The true beginning of my new life will start then."

"Yeah, just be careful," he said. As much as Pippa's security had been a pain in his backside, the fact that she'd had it had given him a measure of relief.

"Oh dear, you're sounding just a bit like Stefan," she said.

"Cut me some slack. I can be protective, too," he said.

She nodded. "I know. It's not totally bad when not taken to extremes," she said. "How are your mother and father?"

"Dad is getting stronger. Mom is getting weaker. It's going to be tricky keeping my dad occupied," he said.

She frowned. "Do I need to take him on an outing?"

Nic chuckled at the image of Pippa taking his dad to the knitting store or brunch. "Nah, I'll just get Goldie to wear him out with some extra workouts."

She nodded. "And what about you?" she asked and he felt as if she were turning a searchlight on his insides.

"I'm good," he said with a shrug.

"You lie, but I understand," she said and squeezed his arm. "I'm sorry this is so hard for you, but you wouldn't be the man I—" She broke off. "You wouldn't be the man I admire you if it weren't hard for you."

"Yeah, well," he said and picked her up off her feet.

Her eyes widened. "What are you doing?"

"Just checking your weight. Making sure you're not wasting away without a chef."

She laughed. "I'm not suffering that much," she said.

He pulled her against him and slid her down the

front of him. "I'm headed out of town tomorrow. Can you come over tonight?"

She nodded.

He felt a rush of relief. "I'll send Goldie to pick you up. Wear this and you'll be fine."

Pippa groaned. "As soon as my security guy retires, I'm burning the wig."

"Don't rush it. You never know when you'll need it."

"Where are you headed?"

"Back to the States for business and one personal mission. Let's go see my mom. She'll fuss if she knows I kept you from going inside," he said.

Pippa saw the weariness stamped on Amelie's face. Nic's mother tried to hide it, but it was unmistakable. Still, Amelie seemed happy to see her and Pippa promised to visit with her the following day. Not wanting to tire her further, Pippa gave the woman a hug and left. Nic walked her to the dreadful machine that was her covert car.

"I'll see you later," he said, pulling her against him. His strength tugged at her. She didn't know how he kept everything together. She just longed to help him as much as she could.

"Later," she promised and kissed him, then drove away.

Hours later, she ate a frozen dinner and tried to play catch-up with her academic work. First, she waited for her security detail to leave for the evening, then she waited for Goldie's call. Her stomach danced with nerves on her way to see Nic.

The more time she spent with Nic, the more she felt

as if she were making a commitment toward him. With the way her family felt about the Lafittes, she just didn't see how anything between her and Nic could end well. Pippa closed her eyes against the thoughts. She couldn't think past tonight. There was too much to work out and she knew she couldn't do it all at once.

But she could be with Nic tonight, hold him and treasure the way she felt when she was with him, the way she felt in his arms.

When Goldie pulled into the driveway, he immediately got out and opened the door for her. "Your Highness," he said with a dip of his head.

"Thank you, Goldie," she said. "But I already told you to call me Pippa."

"Yes, you're welcome, Your—" The big man broke off and smiled. "Your Pippa," he said.

She smiled. He was such a gentle giant.

"I'll take you home whenever you like," he said. "Enjoy your evening."

Pippa walked the few steps to the guest suite and lifted her hand to knock on the door, but it opened before she had a chance.

Nic caught her hand and pulled her inside. "What took you so long?"

"I waited for my security detail to go home," she said.

"Good for you," he said. "Have you had dinner?"

She nodded. "As a matter of fact, I have."

"Are you going to tell me what you ate?"

She shook her head. "No."

He chuckled. "That tells me enough. Goldie put together some appetizers and he baked a pie."

"A pie?" she echoed. "Is there anything he can't do?"

"Not much," he said. "Have a seat. I'll get you a glass of wine."

They shared easy conversation while they ate the appetizers. Pippa was almost too full for pie.

"The proper way to eat this apricot pie is with ice cream," Nic said.

"À la mode," she said. "But I can't imagine eating a full slice."

"Then we can share," he said and scooped up a bite for her. The gesture was both generous and sensual.

"Delicious again," she said. "What time do you leave tomorrow?"

"We're not going to talk about tomorrow, but I'm leaving around 5:00 a.m."

Pippa gasped. "You should go to bed and I should leave. You need to get your rest."

"I can sleep on the flight, but I like your idea of going to bed," he said, his dark gaze wrapping around hers and holding tight.

She took a last sip of her wine and met his challenge. "Then what are you waiting for?"

He immediately took her hand and led her to the bed. He skimmed his hand over her crazy, curly hair. "I didn't expect to want you this much after the first time we were together," he said, kissing her. "How can I want you more?"

Her heart hammered in her chest. "I hope I'm not the only one who feels this way," she whispered. "It's almost too much."

"I know," he said. "I've never felt this way before."

"That's a relief," she said and tugged at his shirt.

"Maybe for you. It's hell for me," he said, and began to undress her.

They kissed and caressed each other into a frenzy. He made her breathless and she did the same to him. Finally he filled her and they stared into each other's eyes.

Pippa wasn't sure if it took seconds or moments later. She only knew she felt taken all the way to her soul.

"I want you," he muttered. "I need you. I—"

He didn't finish, but she craved the words, the emotion, everything that he was. Her heart and stomach clenched, and she arched toward him as he thrust deeply inside her.

Her climax sent her soaring.

"It's never enough," he said. "I can't get enough of you."

Thank goodness, she thought and wrapped herself around him from head to toe. She clung to him with every fiber of her being, wanting him to draw her strength into him.

"I want you with me," he said next to her ear. "All the time."

*Love me,* she thought. *Love me just for me, that's all I want.* She wished he would say, *I'll take care of you forever.* The thought took her by surprise. Pippa didn't want to be the one taken care of. She wanted to be the woman strong enough to stand up and take care of her man and give him anything he needed from her.

"I want to be with you anytime," Pippa whispered. "Every time."

They made love again and afterward, Pippa realized that Nic needed rest. He might deny it, but the truth was he needed rest. She knew he needed far more rest than he could possibly get tonight.

Relaxed against him, Pippa fought sleep. "I need to go back to my apartment."

Nic swore. "I wanted to talk you into staying here all night."

"It will be easier for you to rest tonight, then wake up to leave tomorrow without me here," she said.

"Says who?" he said.

"Says me," she said and lifted her hand to stroke his forehead. "You have a tough trip ahead of you. Business and something else you're not telling me."

He leaned his head back and narrowed his eyes. "How do you know?" he challenged.

"I just do," she said. "Besides, you said you had a personal mission, too."

He scowled at her, then chuckled. "I'm going to bring my brothers back. Even if I have to kidnap them."

Pippa gasped, then bit her lip. "Well, bloody hell, if anyone can do it, you can."

He laughed louder this time and put his hands on either side of her hand as if she were the most precious thing in the universe.

"If you get arrested," she began.

"Would you pay my bail?" he asked.

"Oh, yes," she said without a second thought. She squeezed his hands. "Call me anytime," she told Nic.

"I will, unless a police officer does…asking you to make bail," he said and gave a dry chuckle.

"You're a bad, bad boy with an amazing heart," she said.

"That's why you fell for me from the beginning," he said.

She bit her lip. "Yeah, maybe. Just promise me you'll take care of you," she said.

"I will. Spend some time with my mother," he said. "She's on the edge and I have a feeling you could bring her away from it."

Surprised at his belief in her ability, she shook her head. "I'll visit her tomorrow, but you know I can't control her future."

"Yeah," he said. "I think being with you makes things better for her."

"I'll do my best," she promised. "My very best."

Pippa reluctantly dragged herself from Nic's bed and washed her face and pulled on her clothes. Stepping out of the bathroom, she felt Nic step behind her and wrap his arms around her. "What are you doing?"

"Drawing your life force into me," he said.

She giggled. "That sounds ominous if it were possible."

"How do you know it's not?" he asked.

"I'm taking a wild guess," she said, turning in his arms.

"Well, damn," he said.

"Well, damn," she echoed, and they kissed. She caressed his mouth and squeezed his body tight. "Kick your brothers' asses down the street like a can and bring them here to Chantaine."

He drew back to meet her gaze. "That's pretty strong language for a princess," he said.

"Just sayin'," she said.

"How cool are you?" he said. "I'll get the job done.

Thanks for sticking with me," he said with a gaze that held all kinds of crazy emotions she was determined to ignore but couldn't. "I'll see you soon," he said.

She kissed him and headed toward the door. "*Ciao, darling*," she said. "Be safe."

Goldie drove her home even though it was 2:00 a.m. He didn't even blink at the time. Pippa took a deep breath and leaned her head back against the seat. "You're kind to drive me back to the apartment at such a crazy hour."

He shrugged. "Crazy is relative," he said.

"You're quite amazing," she said. "With all your skills. Nic and I ate your appetizers and a few bites of your amazing pie last night."

"Cooking relaxes me. I'm glad you enjoyed the food I prepared," he said.

"It was delicious. Is there anything that helps you relax? You spend so much of your time working," she said.

Goldie took a deep breath. "I'm addicted to yoga."

"Really?" Pippa asked. "Does it make that much of a difference?"

"Yes," Goldie said. "Relieves pain, allows me to relax and sleep."

"Do you go to a special studio?" she asked.

"Sometimes," he said. "Otherwise, I use a DVD or cable on TV."

"What station?" she asked.

He smiled. "Eight. You can DVR it. Meditation and acupuncture can help, too."

Pippa thought about the prospect of having needles

stuck inside her and shook her head. "If you say so," she said.

"Take it slow. You will learn your truth," he said.

"Goldie, what do you think of this whole crazy situation with me, Nic, Amelie and Paul?" she said.

"You're more powerful than you know," he said.

She thought about that for a moment. "I hope so, but speaking of power—you are quite powerful and talented. Why do you stay with the Lafittes?" she asked.

"They are my home," he said. "I would do anything for them."

His resolute statements sent chills through her. "I wish I had your talent and your fortitude," she said.

"You have both," he said. "Don't fear them."

Goldie pulled into her apartment complex, flashing a pass, then driving toward her apartment. "I'll escort you upstairs," he said.

"It's not necessary," she said.

"It is for me," he said, pulling to a stop. Stepping outside the car, he opened her door and walked with her to her second-floor apartment. "I'll wait outside. Knock on the door to let me know you're okay."

Pippa ventured inside her apartment. For just a half beat, she felt lonely and insecure. Then she gave a quick walk-through to her bedroom. She realized she was okay and opened the door. "No one here but me," she said to Goldie. "Perhaps I should get a cat."

Goldie chuckled. "Good night, Your Highness," he said.

Pippa spent most of the next day with Amelie. Nic's mother knitted, chatted and dozed on and off throughout the day. Pippa noticed that Amelie's energy came and went in short spurts. Paul lumbered restlessly on crutches. Nic had been correct about his father's need to release pent-up energy. Goldie stepped in and helped occupy Paul.

Pippa remembered Amelie when she'd had so much more energy. She'd been so lively, engaging. Irresistible. She still possessed her charm even when sleeping. Her stubby eyelashes rimmed her eyes. Her face growing more gaunt every day, full of wrinkles, crinkles, hollows and bones, defined her character. Her stubborn chin told the world she would push it to the max, till the very end. Amelie was nothing if not a fighter.

Pippa felt her throat suddenly close shut at the realization that Amelie was going to die, and it would be soon. She'd known all along that Amelie's time was short, but Pippa realized she'd been in denial. Amelie's time was all too close. Pippa left a little later than she'd planned. Goldie gave her a sandwich and followed her home.

Pippa took a shower and fell into a dreamless sleep. She awakened to the sound of her cell phone beeping. Glancing at the caller ID, she saw that Bridget was on the line.

Reluctantly, she accepted the call. "Good morning, Bridget. How are you?"

"When did you move? Why didn't you tell me? I went to your suite and you weren't there. Stefan won't discuss it, but he's clearly furious. How could you do this to us?"

"I moved a few days ago. It took place quickly because I had to do it before I lost my courage. I couldn't continue to live in the palace. I felt so trapped," Pippa said.

"We all feel trapped," Bridget scoffed. "The key is stealing your freedom whenever you can."

"You're a better fighter than I am," Pippa said. "I needed to finish the big fight so there could be peace for me, for everyone."

Silence stretched between them. Bridget gave an audible sigh. "I want to argue with you, but I can't. I obviously haven't had enough coffee." She gave a growl of frustration. "Maybe I'm just jealous that you got out before I did."

Pippa smiled. "You're right on my heels with your ranch in sight. You have Ryder and your boys. I have… genealogy."

"I still may find a man for you," Bridget said.

"Oh, please. If you love me, Bridget, stop," she said and laughed.

"Everyone deserves a second chance," Bridget said.

"Maybe in five years," Pippa said.

"That was cruel," her sister said. "Don't forget, there's a family dinner tonight."

"Lovely," Pippa said. "I'll have the whole table glowering at me."

"Don't be late," Bridget said. "*Ciao,* darling."

## Chapter Eleven

"I want to go to the ocean," Amelie said at three-thirty.

Pippa blinked. "The ocean?" Today had been a duplicate of yesterday with Amelie knitting, chatting and sleeping except for this latest request.

"Yes, I want to swim," Amelie said, standing. "I'll put on my suit."

Pippa followed the woman to her feet. "I'm not sure that's wise. I don't think you're supposed to be swimming."

"Why not?" Amelie asked.

"Well, because of your condition," Pippa said.

"Oh, you mean the draining procedure. I'm permitted to swim after five days. I don't suppose you have a suit. I'm not sure mine would fit. Perhaps I should go by myself."

*No.* "I'll come up with something. Goldie can help me," Pippa said. "Go change into your suit." She wondered if Amelie would tire before they were able to leave. As soon as Amelie walked down the hallway, Pippa called for Goldie. Somehow she ended up with shorts and a tank top.

With surprising energy, Amelie returned wearing a caftan, the strap of her swimsuit peeking through the shoulder sliding over her too-slim frame. "Ready to be a little fish?" she asked with a singsong tone in her voice.

"Ready," Pippa said. "Goldie said he'll drive us."

Amelie frowned. "But what about Paul?"

"He's already given Paul a good workout. Paul is napping in the extra room," Pippa said.

"Excellent," Amelie said. "Let's go. Another adventure."

Heaven help them all, Pippa thought. Moments later, they trudged through the sandy beach toward the ocean. Partway there, Amelie pulled her caftan over her head and dropped her towel on the sand. She lifted her head to the sun and smiled like a child.

Pippa's heart caught. She picked up her cell phone and clicked a photo and another. She was no photographer, but she hoped the photos somehow captured Amelie's love of life.

"Let's go," Amelie called. "Before the water gets too cold."

Pippa tossed her cell phone into her bag and ran toward the ocean with Nic's mother. The water was already cold. Pippa muffled a shriek. "It's a bit nippy."

"Could be worse," Amelie said. "We're lucky it's not winter. The waves are so calm."

Amelie reached for Pippa's hand. "Isn't it lovely?"

Pippa took a deep breath and looked at the beautiful

blue ocean with the slightest caps of white. Both she and Amelie wore water shoes to cushion them from the rocky ground.

Amelie smiled but her teeth chattered. "I always wanted to be a fish or a dolphin," she said. "Or a butterfly."

"You're all of those in one," she said.

Amelie laughed. Her lips were turning blue. "You're such a lovely person. The perfect princess." Her smile fell. "The one thing I'll miss is meeting my grandchildren. You could have my first grandchild."

Pippa stared at Amelie in shock. "Grandchild?" she echoed. She felt her insides clench. Could Amelie sense something? In fact, she was late with her period, but because she wasn't regular, pregnancy wasn't a concern. Nic had worn protection.

"Don't worry, it will all work out. You'll have a beautiful baby," Amelie said.

Pippa wondered for a moment if Nic's mother was suffering from some kind of delusion. "You've grown cold. We should go back."

"Just a moment longer," she said. "I want to feel the water and the waves a moment longer."

Pippa laced her fingers more tightly through Amelie's and began to count. She was torn between protecting Amelie's pleasure and her fragile health. Amelie stumbled, then dipped her shoulders underneath the water.

"Amelie," Pippa said.

Seconds later, Amelie ducked her head beneath, frightening the bloody hell out of Pippa. She tugged on Amelie's hand, pulling her above the surface. "What are you doing?" she asked Nic's mother.

"It was so nice under the water," Amelie said, beaming. "I feel like I'm nine years old again."

Pippa put her arms around Amelie and squeezed her tight. "Let's get our towels. I want you cozy and warm."

Amelie's teeth chattered as Pippa led her to their towels. Goldie rushed out to help them into the car. "Turn on the heat, please," Pippa said.

"But it's—" Goldie broke off and met Pippa's gaze. Understanding flowed between them. For Amelie, it may as well have been winter. Her body was so thin and she'd become chilled in the water.

"I hope she won't get sick from this," Pippa said, scrubbing Amelie's arms.

"She won't," Goldie said. "You did the right thing, Your Highness. She was determined to go to the sea. We're lucky you went with her."

They returned to the cottage and Pippa helped Amelie into cozy pajamas, then into bed. Only after Goldie's promise to frequently check on Amelie did Pippa agree to leave. As she climbed into cab, she noticed the time. Bloody hell. She was going to be late for the family dinner.

Rushing, rushing, rushing, she took a shower, dressed herself and pulled her errant hair into a bun. Forget cosmetics, she told herself. She drove to the palace and raced up to the private dining room and burst inside. Everyone was there, her brother, his child and his pregnant wife, Eve, her sister Bridget, her husband, Ryder, and the twins. For one stunning moment, they were silent. Damn them.

"Hi," she said, forcing a big smile. "I'm so sorry I'm late. Time got away from me." She sank into the empty seat. "How are you feeling, Eve?"

Eve shot her a look of sympathy. "Better, thank you. How are your studies?"

"I'm getting there," Pippa said and glanced at Bridget. "How's the ranch?"

"Well, if we could get the plumbing and the kitchen straight, we'd be most of the way there," Bridget said. "Why is your hair wet?"

"I just took a shower," Pippa said and reached for her glass of water. She eyed the wine, but remembering what Amelie said, she wasn't sure she should do much drinking. She didn't think she was pregnant, but she supposed it was remotely possible.

Her hand shook as she held the glass of water. *Pregnant? No.*

"What's for dinner?" she asked brightly.

"Beef, rare," Eve said, wincing slightly. "Stefan's favorite."

"Mashed potatoes for Eve and anyone else who wants them. It's the only thing she can eat. That, and bread."

With the help of her screaming niece and nephews, Pippa made it through the meal. She gave a sigh of relief as dessert was served. Bananas flambé served with a flourish. She took a few bites, then discreetly motioned for one of the servers to take her plate.

"This had been wonderful, but I should leave. Back to work early tomorrow," she said and pushed back her chair.

"I'd like a word with you," Stefan said. "In my office."

"Our suite," Eve said. "Stephenia would love a bed-time hug and kiss from her aunt Pippa."

A flicker of irritation crossed his face, but he appeared to mask it with a quick nod. "Our suite will be fine." He said good-night to Bridget and her family, then the four of them made their way to Stefan and Eve's suite. Pippa had noticed Stefan had appeared more remote than usual this evening, but she'd just thought he was either still peeved about her move or his mind was on something else altogether.

Once inside the suite, Pippa kneeled down and extended her arms to Stephenia. "Come give me a big hug."

The little girl rushed toward her, her curls bobbing. Laughing, she threw her little body against Pippa. Her uninhibited expression of joy and complete trust tugged at Pippa's heart. "Now that's a hug," Pippa said and kissed the toddler's soft cheek. "You are such a sweet and smart girl. I bet you've been busy today."

Eve nodded with a wry expression on her face. "There'll be an early bedtime for Mamaeve tonight, too. Come along, Stephenia. You need to pick out your book. And Stefan—" she said but stopped.

Pippa saw the silent communication between the two of them and wondered what was going on. Surely he couldn't still be so upset about her move from the palace.

Stefan brushed a kiss over his daughter's cheek. "Sweet dreams," he said, echoing Eve's frequent night-time wish.

As soon as Eve and Stephenia walked toward the

bedrooms at the other end of the suite, Stefan turned toward Pippa. "How are you?"

"Well, thank you. And you?"

"Also well. Your studies?"

Pippa resisted the urge to squirm. She'd been forced to put her academic work aside during the last week. "Demanding as always."

"You've been quite busy since you returned from Italy," he said. He pulled out a computer tablet and turned it on.

The uneasiness inside her grew. "Moving makes for a busy time." She hesitated to ask but went ahead anyway. "What is your point?"

"Some photographs of you were posted on a social network just before dinner. I'll be surprised if they don't make the rag sheets by morning." He showed her a series of photos of her holding hands with Amelie in the ocean. "The woman looks familiar," he said in a cool voice.

Her stomach knotted, yet at the same time an overwhelming relief swept through her. "Good eye, Your Royal Highness. That's Amelie Lafitte."

Stefan clenched his jaw. "What in hell have you gotten yourself into?"

Pippa sighed. "I got myself involved with a family experiencing a tragedy."

"What tragedy? I'd heard Amelie had been ill for some time, but if she's swimming, she must have recovered."

Pippa shook her head. "Amelie is terminally ill. She's—she's dying."

Surprise crossed his face. "I'm sorry to hear that."

He cleared his throat. "That said, any association with the Lafittes is understandably forbidden. You must stop your involvement at once."

Pippa shook her head. "Oh, I'm sorry. That's not possible."

Stefan tilted his head to one side in disbelief and disapproval. "Pardon me, of course it's possible. You merely send a message to the Lafittes with your good wishes, but tell them you're unable to continue the association."

"I can't and won't do that. At this time of all times, I would hate myself for pulling away from them."

Stefan's jaw tightened again. "Pippa, after I received these photos, I asked my security detail to investigate the situation with the Lafittes. It has been brought to my attention that you've used family connections to secure a cottage for them. Not only that, Paul Lafitte, whose presence in this country is illegal, is living in this cottage. How do you think your cousin Georgina will feel when she learns you've used her cottage to house a criminal?"

"He's not a criminal," she said, unable to fight a stab of impatience. "He's a man with a broken foot and he's about to lose the love of his life."

"Pippa, this is not up for discussion. What you've done is illegal and dishonest."

"I'm not proud of being dishonest with all of you. I've hated every one of the lies I've had to tell, but your attitude made it impossible."

"I don't think you understand what a black mark this will make on our name. I insist you sever your relationship with the Lafittes," he said. "Please don't force my hand on this."

Pippa fought a sliver of fear, but her anger at his manipulation was stronger. "Are you threatening me? With what? Let's not keep it a mystery."

He paused, then narrowed his eyes. "If you don't stop your association with the Lafittes, I'll be forced to consider revoking your title."

Pippa absorbed the potential loss and made her decision in less than two breaths. "Then do what you have to do. I'll do what I must do. Helping the Lafittes through this painful time is the most important thing I've ever done in my life. If I lose my title over it, then c'est la vie. Good night, Stefan," she said and walked out of his suite.

Her heels clicked against the familiar marble palace floor. It crossed her mind that if Stefan carried through with his threat, this might be the last time she walked these halls. Worse yet, she realized, she might lose her relationship with her family. Her chest tightened with grief. Her hands began to shake and she balled them into fists. As much as her dysfunctional family drove each other crazy at times, Pippa loved them with all her heart. She would never get over losing them.

Deep in her heart, though, she knew that she would hate herself if she turned her back on the Lafittes. Stefan had forced her to make an impossible choice. She prayed she would have the strength to live with the consequences.

The connecting flight from Madrid began its descent into Chantaine just after 8:00 a.m. Nic rubbed his eyes, which felt like sandpaper. He looked at the passengers beside him and behind him. By some miracle, all three of his brothers were on the flight. Alex, his youngest brother, sat beside him gently snoring. Paul Jr., who went by James, and Michael sat across the aisle in the row behind them.

The plane had a bumpy landing. Nic hoped it wasn't a sign of what was to come for the rest of his brothers' visit.

Alex awakened, rubbing his face. He narrowed his eyes at Nic. "Looks like we made it. Are you sure our father isn't in a Chantaine dungeon somewhere?"

"You never know with Paul Lafitte, but he wasn't when I left," Nic said. "Besides, you're not here to see your father. You're here to see your mother," Nic said. "If you're man enough."

Alex scowled, but Nic knew that very same challenge had gotten Alex and Nic's other brothers onto the plane. He'd made a strong, no-holds-barred demand, and thank goodness, his brothers had responded.

"There's a car waiting," Nic said. "When we get to the cottage, you'll have a good meal."

An hour later, the driver drove the limo toward the cottage. The ride was mostly silent, but Nic figured he would be paying the price for the intimidation and manipulation he'd used to bring his brothers to his mother. Despite their anger, their brothers drank in the sight of their mother's island.

"Not bad," James said. "Never visited Chantaine before. Mom always said it was beautiful. She was right."

Alex gave a dry chuckle. "Who says they would have let us on the island?"

"You got on this time," Nic said.

"Because you've donated a ton of money and enhanced Chantaine's economy," Alex said.

"There are worse ways to spend money," Nic said.

The limo pulled into the driveway.

"Quaint," Paul Jr. said.

"A friend helped out," Nic said. He wondered how Pippa was doing. He knew that moving from the palace was a huge change for her. He and his brothers got out of the limo and walked to the front door.

Paul opened the door. On crutches, he looked at his four sons in shock. "Well, I'll be damned."

"We've already done that several times over," Paul Jr. said. "Where's Mom?"

Paul's expression hardened. "She's asleep, and if you can't show her respect and kindness, you can go the hell back where you came from," he said and slammed the door in their faces.

Silence followed.

"Same ol' dad," Michael said.

"Yep, sonofabitch, but he was always protective of her," Alex said.

"When he wasn't in prison," Paul Jr. said.

"This is stupid," Nic said. "Let's just go inside. Dad will have to deal with it. I'm sure Goldie has a great meal for us."

"Who's Goldie?" Paul Jr. asked.

"You'll know soon enough," Nic said and inserted his key into the door and pushed it open.

Paul had apparently hobbled to the back of the house. Nic turned on a baseball game and Goldie immediately showed up with platters of appetizers and sandwiches, along with beer. Beer before lunch may have seemed inappropriate, but in this case, it was for the best. His brothers commented on the food and the game while downing a few beers.

Finally, his mother appeared in the back of the den. "She's here," Nic said, turning off the TV. His mother was gaunt and tired, but clearly delighted to see her sons.

"Am I dreaming?" she asked, lifting her lips in a huge smile.

"Go," Nic said in his brother Michael's ear.

"Me?" Michael asked.

Nic nodded, and half a breath later, Michael sprang to his feet and enveloped his mother in hug. "I'm sorry I haven't—"

"No sorries, no apologies," Amelie said, hugging him in return. "I'm so happy to see you."

A moment later, James rose and pulled her into his arms. "Mom, I've missed you."

Alex finally stood and made his way to his mother. "I'm the worst of your sons," he confessed.

"No," she insisted with a smile. "You are all the best sons any woman could want because you came to see me before—" She broke off, her smile fading. "Before I turn into a butterfly."

Nic's heart wrenched at the sight before him. It had taken an enormous effort to make this happen. He just wished it hadn't been necessary.

His mother pretended to eat and sipped some lemonade while she enjoyed the visit with her sons. Amelie asked each of them about what they were doing. None were married and none had children, much to her disappointment. She encouraged all of them to enjoy Chantaine as much as possible during their visit, but Nic knew his brothers were leaving at 5:00 a.m. the next day.

After a while, Nic could tell she was growing tired. "We should let you rest," he said.

"In a bit. I have something to say first," she said. "You're not going to like this, but I raised you to be extraordinary men, so now's the time for you to man up."

The room turned silent. His brothers grew restless.

"Take a deep breath. Listen. It won't be that long. You can handle it," she said. "The truth is your father broke the rules because he was determined to take care of me. He was determined to keep me in the same way a princess should live because, after all, I could have been a princess. How do you compete with that? How do you produce a lifestyle fit for a princess, even though I didn't ask for it?"

His mother's words sank into him. He'd never realized what a burden his father had taken on when he'd stolen his mother from Prince Edward. It made him think of his current relationship with Pippa.

"Can't deny that was tough," James said. "But he made our life a living hell by destroying the family reputation."

"True," his mother said. "But that was a long time ago. It's time to get over it."

Silence followed.

"Excuse me?" Michael said. "Get over it? His disreputable dealings are the gifts that keep giving. We had to move out of the state to reestablish ourselves."

"Well," his mother said. "It's time for you to get over it. You've reestablished yourselves. Paul is nursing a broken foot. I have two things to ask of you," she said. "Be true brothers. Stand together. Be family. And forgive your father," she added.

Nic felt his brothers close up like locks at Fort Knox. "Love you, Mom," he said and moved toward her to give her a hug.

She embraced him in return. "Thank you," she said. "You made a miracle."

"No, it was you," he said. "I just added a little muscle."

"I'm getting tired. I should go to sleep. Can we get a photo of me with my boys?" she asked.

Goldie took a few photos and his mother went to bed. His brothers sacked out in the guest room and guest quarters. Nic considered calling Pippa, but he was drained. He resolved to call tomorrow afternoon, after his brothers left and he caught up with some rest.

Nic arranged for the limo that took his brothers to the airport in the early predawn morning, then went back to sleep. Hours later, a knock on the door awakened him. Goldie, wearing a tortured expression, dipped his head. "I'm so sorry, sir. Your mother has passed on."

## Chapter Twelve

Numb from the news, Nic dialed Pippa's number as he paced his room an hour later.

"Hi. Welcome back," she said.

Her voice was like oxygen to his system. "Thanks," he said. "I have some bad news." He paused a beat because he'd already had to say the same thing several times. "She's gone."

"Oh, Nic, I'm so sorry. I'll be right over," she said.

"Good," he said, feeling a shot of relief that bothered him. Now, more than ever, he needed to keep himself in check. There was just too much to do and his father was a mess.

He made several more calls, unsure what to do about a memorial service. Thank goodness, his mother had made her burial wishes clear in her will. She wanted her ashes spread in Chantaine. Nic suspected his father would fight it.

He heard a vehicle pull into the driveway and immediately went to the door. Pippa stepped from the car and rushed into his arms. "I'm so sorry. How are you?" she asked.

Feeling her in his arms was a balm to his soul. "I'm okay. We knew this was coming."

"But you're never really ready," she said, pulling back to search his face.

"True, but we were more prepared than most," he said and led her into the den.

"How is your father?" she asked.

"Not good," Nic said. "He was having some pain with his foot, so he spent the whole night on the patio. My brothers were sleeping in the guestroom. I think my father must have taken an extra dose of pain reliever because he didn't even wake up when my brothers left early this morning. Goldie went in to take her a croissant and some juice. He was the one who found her. My father was horrified that she died alone." His throat closed up.

Pippa took his hand in hers. "But your brothers, did she see them?"

Nic nodded.

"It's almost as if she was waiting to see them again and that gave her permission. You did a wonderful thing by bringing them here," she said.

"Trust me, I had to be damn ugly to them to make it happen," he said.

"And now there are other things to be done. Arrangements," she said. "How can I help you?"

Nic took a deep breath. "I need one more favor. My mother wanted her ashes spread here in Chantaine."

"And a memorial service, too," she said, her eyebrows furrowing together in concern.

"Yeah," he said.

"I'll do my best. Not sure Stefan is speaking to me at the moment," she added in half jest.

"Why? Is he still upset that you moved out of the palace?" Nic demanded.

Pippa waved her hand in a dismissive gesture. "Stefan's always bothered about something. It's his nature. What about your brothers? You said they'd already left."

"They're on their way back," he said. "I'd like to do this quickly and get my father back to the States. There are too many sad memories for him here and he's going to have to find a new normal for himself."

Pippa nodded. "Okay, I'll go out by the pool area and make a few calls," she said and left him to his list.

Fifteen minutes later, she returned, relief on her face. "I was able to get permission for your mother's service. Because the weather has been good, I wondered if you would like it to take place outdoors. There's a lovely green park on the other side of the island that people use for all kinds of occasions including memorial services. Chairs can be set up for your family."

"That sounds good. Thank you," he said, mentally checking the decision off his list. Nic felt as if he had a million-mile journey in front of him. Pippa made everything feel easier, but soon enough, he would be back in the States and he would be handling everything by himself. Again.

Two days later, Pippa took a seat at the end of a second row of chairs arranged for Amelie Lafitte's memorial service. She didn't want to call attention to herself. By a stroke of luck, or fate, she'd located a minister who had lived in the same orphanage as Amelie. She was pleased that someone who had known Nic's mother would lead the service.

It was a beautiful morning. Amelie would have loved it.

"Excuse me, is that seat taken?" a familiar voice asked her.

Pippa looked up and surprise raced through at the sight of her sister-in-law, Eve, and her sister Bridget. She stood, feeling as if her heart would burst with gratitude. "I don't know what to say," she said. "I can't believe you're here."

"Of course we're here. You're family. This is where we're supposed to be. Stefan didn't come because he didn't want to turn things into a madhouse," Eve said. "But he sends his condolences to you and the Lafittes."

Pippa hugged Eve. "You must have given him a Texas-size lecture because the last I heard, I no longer had a title," she said.

Bridget rolled her eyes. "He's got to make that threat to each of us at some point. He just can't stand not having control sometimes, most times," she added and held out her arms. "Come here. Shame on you for suffering by yourself. Why can't you be more like me and make everyone suffer with you?"

Bridget's remark made her laugh despite how emotional she felt. "I knew none of you would approve," Pippa said. "But I couldn't turn my back on them."

"That's one of the many reasons we love you," Eve said as she took her seat. Bridget also took hers.

Within the next moments, many people arrived, taking seats and crowding around the area. "I didn't know this many people remembered Amelie," Bridget said, surprised at the number of people gathering in the park.

"You would understand if you'd met her. I wish you'd had the opportunity," Pippa said, her eyes suddenly filling with tears. "She was a magical person."

Bridget covered her hand in comfort and the Lafitte men arrived, filing into the front row of chairs reserved for Amelie's family. Seconds later, the minister stood at the front of the group and began to speak.

He delivered a heartfelt message with touches of humor as he described Amelie as a child and how she seemed to have held on to her sense of wonder despite life's trials. Nic then read a message his mother had written for the occasion. The sight of him so strong delivering his mother's last words wrenched at her. She knew he had to be suffering but wouldn't reveal it. Pippa wished with all her heart that she could help him.

As the service drew to a close, Pippa noticed Bebe, the proprietor of Amelie's favorite creperie, move toward the front of the crowd. "Please forgive the interruption, but Amelie was such a joy. We were so thrilled to receive a visit from her a short time ago and she was just as beautiful as ever. Several of us who knew her have asked and received permission to plant some buddleia in her honor. We've planted one already. It's over there," Bebe said, pointing to the flowering bush to the left of the crowd.

Eve gave a loud sniff. "Now that could make even me cry. A butterfly bush."

"And look," Bridget said. "There are butterflies."

Pippa saw the beautiful butterflies fluttering and met Nic's knowing gaze. Amelie had often said she wanted to be a butterfly. In that moment, she felt the bond between Nic and her solidify. They would always remember, together.

Nic asked her to come to the cottage after the service. She had arranged for a catering service to bring food. With all the turmoil of the past few days, Nic, his brothers and his father might have forgotten to eat, but their hunger would remind them soon enough. When she arrived, they were silently eating. Nic introduced her to his brothers and they all responded politely. Moments later, they all scattered except Nic.

"It was a beautiful service. I believe Amelie would have approved," she said.

"Yeah, especially with those butterflies. That caught me by surprise," he said, shoving one of his hands into his pocket. He'd pulled off his necktie and opened his shirt. Dark circles rimmed his eyes. Pippa knew he hadn't gotten much sleep.

"What else can I do for you?" she asked.

He pulled her into his arms. "Oh, hell, Pippa, you've already done more than I could imagine. The rest is up to me. I'll pack up my dad and we'll head out tomorrow."

Surprise rushed through her. She'd known he planned to leave soon, but not this soon. "Tomorrow?"

"Yeah, I need to get him away from Chantaine. I'll send in a team to clean up the cottage," he said.

"I can make those arrangements," she said.

"No, you've already done enough. Too much," he

said and sighed. "When I said fate would bring you and me together, I had no idea it would be for this. Or that it would turn out this way."

Pippa felt a twist of nerves at his words. "What do you mean 'turn out this way'?"

"Well, I've got to leave now. I've got to get my dad straight. There's no one else to do it," he said.

Alarm shot through her. "Are you saying goodbye?"

"No. I'm just saying I'm not free to be here with you right now. When I get my Dad settled, we'll see if you're still interested," he said.

Pippa stared at him in disbelief. "Of course I'll still be interested. Why wouldn't I be?"

"Your family still hates the Lafittes," he said. "In their eyes, I'll never be good enough for you."

"My family is rethinking their stance on the Lafittes. Besides, what's important is how I feel about you, not how they feel about you."

"We'll see, darlin'. You've taken a lot of heat for me. You deserve a break to decide if I'm worth the trouble," he said.

"But, Nic," she began and he covered her mouth with his index finger.

"Trust me. This is for the best," he said and lowered his mouth to kiss her.

Two weeks later when Pippa hadn't heard from Nic, she wasn't at all sure this *break,* or whatever Nic called it, was for the best. Plus, there was the matter of her increasingly regular nausea. When she counted the number of days since her last menstrual period, she broke into a sweat and got sick to her stomach again.

Even though she'd known she was late a couple weeks ago, she figured it was due to stress. After all, Nic had always used protection. So nothing could happen, right? The combination of her symptoms and that strange conversation she'd had with Amelie just before Nic's mother had died gnawed at her.

It took several more days for Pippa to work up the nerve to take a pregnancy test. She even dragged out the old disguise of the hated gray wig and ugly clothes and paid cash at the pharmacy so that no one would recognize her. She nearly fainted at the result. Positive. Perhaps she should get another test. She did, three of them, actually, from different pharmacies. The results were all positive.

She knew she needed to tell Nic, but this wasn't the kind of news she could give over the phone. It wasn't as if she could send a cheery little text saying *Guess who's going to be a daddy?* She knew he must be terribly busy making up for lost time with his businesses and helping his father create a new life, but the lack of contact from him only fueled questions and doubts inside her.

She and Nic had never discussed marriage, and she really didn't like the idea of him proposing just because she was pregnant. She wanted Nic to propose marriage because he didn't want to live without her.

Pippa rolled her eyes at herself. As if Nic Lafitte would ever allow himself to want a woman that much.

Suffering more and more each passing day, she avoided her family. Her older sister Valentina may have gotten pregnant without the benefit of marriage, but she'd had the good sense not to tell Stefan until she was on another continent. Pippa didn't want to even think about how to break the news to her brother.

She plunged herself into her studies and made progress that impressed even her. At the rate she was going, she could wrap up the last of her dissertation within a couple months. She wondered if she would be showing then. Another week passed and she hadn't heard from Nic. What did this mean? Had he forgotten her? The possibility made her ill. What if this had just been a fling for him? What if he hadn't fallen as deeply for her as she had for him? What if she was truly alone? And now with a baby on the way… Even with all the hours she'd been putting in for her dissertation, she was sleeping for only a few hours each night. She avoided looking in the mirror because she knew she was looking more tired and miserable with each passing day.

Pippa had successfully begged off two family dinners, but when Stefan called for an official meeting of all adult Devereauxs, she could no longer hide. The meeting was held in Stefan's office, which indicated potentially serious business. As Pippa entered the office, she noted the additional chairs. Bridget, her older sister Ericka, who lived in Paris, and her younger brother, Jacques, who'd responded to Stefan's missive by leaving his soccer team mid-tour. Ericka and Jacques were both talking on their cell phones.

"Pippa, there you are," Bridget said, then frowned at her. "Oh, my goodness, you look dreadful. What have you been doing to yourself? You need to let me set up a day at the spa for you."

"I've just been trying to make up time on my dissertation. Burning the midnight oil," she said.

"Well, don't burn any more. How are the Lafittes?" Bridget asked. "I apologize for not calling sooner. I've been so busy with the building of our ranch and both the twins got sick."

"I know you're busy. Nic and his father have gone back to the States. They both had a lot to do after Amelie's death," she said.

"Hmm," Bridget said, her mind clearly whirling. "He's been in touch, though, hasn't he? He hasn't just abandoned you after you helped his family."

"He hasn't abandoned me," Pippa said, even though she felt that way. "He's just terribly busy right now. Do you know why Stefan has called the meeting?"

"No," Bridget said.

"It must be big if he insisted that both Jacques and I come immediately," Ericka said and gave Pippa a hug. "I hope no one is ill."

Jacques turned off his phone and approached his sisters. "We're all here except Valentina. I'm stumped about this one. Stefan can go over the top easier than most, but I don't know—"

He broke off as Stefan and Eve entered the room. His assistant closed the door behind him. "Please be seated," Stefan said, his face, devoid of humor.

Pippa's stomach clenched at his expression.

Stefan gave a heavy sigh and sat on the edge of his desk. "As you all know, our father wasn't perfect. We can be thankful to him for our lives, our positions. Nothing will change that. However, he had a mistress for several years. She was a small-time actress. Her name was Ava London."

Pippa felt a stab of surprise, not that her father had

stepped out on her mother, but that Stefan knew the identity of this woman. She slid a sideways glance at Bridget, whose mouth gaped open.

Stefan gave another heavy sigh. "During their affair, Ava gave birth to two children."

Pippa and her siblings gasped in unison. Her mind whirled at the implications.

Stefan nodded. "According to the advisers, this development shouldn't affect succession. The son, Maxwell Carter, is thirty years old and is living in Australia. The daughter, Coco Jordan, is a—" He cleared his throat. "She's a nanny in Texas."

Pippa felt her stomach roll with the news. She couldn't help thinking about her own unborn child. "What else do we know about them? Did Ava raise them? What—"

Stefan shook his head. "Ava made an agreement with my father. He would support her until her death if she gave her children up for adoption and didn't reveal their existence. Ava passed away two weeks ago and her attorney is determined to follow her wishes, which are to ensure that her children know that they have Devereaux blood."

"Great," Bridget muttered. "This sounds like a public relations nightmare."

"It is," Stefan said. "The two children may also have some rights to an inheritance."

Bridget scoffed. "But they haven't had to perform any duties," she protested. "We've spent our life serving."

"True, but our attorneys have not been able to determine the legalities concerning their inheritance," he said.

Pippa skipped over the money issues. She had tried to be aware of economics ever since Stefan had begun to complain about frivolous costs. Her biggest expense had been the cost of her degree and she'd been fortunate to receive scholarships. "What are they like?"

She felt Bridget stare at her. "What do you mean what are they like? They're illegitimate Devereauxs."

"But they're people, human beings," Pippa said. "She's our half sister. He's our half brother."

Eve met her gaze and smiled, giving her a thumbs-up.

"Leave it to Pippa to bring in the human element," Stefan said and gave a half smile. "Both of Coco Jordan's parents have died. She's finishing her education after taking care of her mother during a terminal illness. Her parents left her no inheritance, so we're not sure how she'll respond to the news that she could gain financially from being a Devereaux. The advisers and public relations staff want to control the release of this information, so we will be inviting her to Chantaine as soon as possible."

*"Mon Dieu,"* Ericka said. "You're going to bring her here? Why will you not pay her off and bury this information?"

"Because in a contemporary media environment, we have learned it's impossible to bury this kind of information. Our goal is to take this distressing news and to somehow make it work for us."

"We call that taking lemons and making lemonade," Eve said in her Texas drawl.

"So what's our new *brother* like?" Jacques asked sarcastically. "Knowing our luck, he's a drug dealer or something."

"Not that bad," Stefan conceded. "His adoptive parents live in Ohio. He graduated with a degree in engineering and has been working in Australia for the past few years." He paused a half beat. "He hasn't responded yet to our communications."

"Has the daughter?" Bridget asked.

"Yes," Stefan said. "But she hasn't yet accepted our invitation to come to Chantaine."

"Do you think this is a strategy to make us give her money?" Jacques asked.

"Jacques," Pippa said, "must you be so suspicious? Maybe this has taken her off guard, too. If she stuck with her mother during an illness, she can't be all bad."

The room turned silent because they all knew that Pippa had just helped the Lafittes during their difficult time. Pippa's stomach continued to churn. The realization that her father had denied his own children hit too close to the bone with her. She hadn't been able to talk to Nic yet. How would he respond to the news about her pregnancy?

Suddenly, her feeling of nausea overwhelmed. "Excuse me, I need to leave," she said and ran for the toilet connected to Nic's office. After she was sick, she splashed her face and mouth with water. Glancing into the mirror, she braced herself for what she would face on the other side of her door.

Taking several deep breaths, Pippa opened the door. All of her siblings were standing, waiting. Bridget crossed her arms over her chest, tapping her foot. "Do you have something you want to tell us?" she asked.

Pippa bit her lip. "Not really," she said.

Eve chuckled and the sound eased something inside her.

Stefan narrowed his eyes. "Pippa," he said.

She sighed. "Eve's not the only one who is pregnant," she said.

Stefan's face turned to granite. "Lafitte," he said in disgust. "I'll make him pay."

Her stomach turned again. "No," she said and raced for the toilet again.

Bless her Texan heart, Eve saved Pippa from a grueling discussion with Stefan. Pippa decided she needed to thank the heavens for Eve on a more regular basis. Eve had come through for her in several critical situations.

Pippa returned home and breathed a sigh of relief. She wished, however, that she would hear something, anything, from Nic. She finally gave in, called his cell and left a message. "Hope you and your father are okay," she said. "I need to talk to you when you get a chance."

Less that twenty-four hours later, she got a return call. When she saw the caller ID, her heart hammered so fast she could hardly breathe, let alone speak. "Hi," she said.

"Hey," he said. "It's been nuts here. My father took too many sleeping pills and he's been in the hospital. He's in rehab right now and I'm working on interim housing for him. How are you?"

How could she top his troubles? "I'm fine. I just thought we should touch base," she said, pacing the small den of her apartment.

A short silence followed. "You sound different. Are you sure you're okay?"

"Yes," she said. "I'm fine."

"I would have called you, but I've been slammed with my dad's issues."

"I understand," she said, adding as much backbone to her voice as she could muster. "I'm sorry he's struggling."

"Yeah. I could have predicted it. The good news is my youngest brother has started checking in on him," Nic said.

"That's wonderful. I know your brothers' relationship with your father has been, well, precarious," she said.

"That's a nice way of saying their relationship with him was in the toilet. Flushed repeatedly," Nic said. "My two other brothers don't appear to give a rip, but Alex is working at it. There's hope anyway."

"That's good," she said. "I'm glad."

Another awkward silence stretched between them. "You sure you're okay?"

"I'm fine," she insisted.

"How are the Devereauxs?" he asked.

"In perfect health," she said.

"Good to hear. Stefan breathing down your throat?" he asked.

"No more than usual," she said.

"I need to go," he said. "I'll call you in a couple of days. I'm glad you called. It's so good to hear your voice."

The call was disconnected and it took several seconds before she began to breathe again. His last words vibrated through her. *It's so good to hear your voice.*

He called and left a message the following day. She missed it, damn it, because she was in a meeting with her professor. Three days after that, there was a knock at her door. She looked out the peephole. It was Nic. Her heart hammered against her rib cage. She felt a jolt of nausea rise from her belly.

"Just a moment," Pippa called. She willed her stomach to calm down. Turning away from the door, she took several breaths and told herself she would get through this. She walked to the door and opened it. "Hi," she said.

"Hi," he said, studying her. "Are you okay? You don't look well," he said.

"It's good to see you, too," she said and headed for the toilet. Moments later, she returned to her small den where Nic stood with a brooding expression on his face.

"You're not sick, are you?" he asked.

"Not really," she said. "I've just had some nausea lately."

He frowned. "That was one of my mother's symptoms," he said.

Her heart softened. "Oh, it's not that. I'm not sick that way, Nic."

"How can you be sure?" he asked.

"I just am. Trust me," she said.

He searched her face for a long moment. "Then what is it?"

She took a deep breath. "Why don't we sit down? Would you like water or ginger ale?"

"Ginger ale," he echoed, clearly disgusted.

"Water," she said and laughed. "Have a seat." She filled two glasses with ice and water and brought them into her small den. Giving one of the glasses to him, she sat across from him. "I didn't expect you."

He took several swallows of water. "I didn't like the way you sounded."

She winced. "How is your father?"

"Okay at the moment. Alex is checking in on him." He set his glass down on a coaster on a lamp table. "What the hell is going on? Something's wrong. If you want to dump me, just say it."

Pippa dropped her jaw in astonishment. "That thought hasn't occurred to me."

"Then why are you acting so weird?" he demanded.

"I wasn't aware that I was acting weird," she said.

"Well, you are," he said.

"We haven't seen each other in nearly a month and we didn't talk for almost three weeks," she pointed out.

"I told you what was happening with my father," he said.

"Yes, but that doesn't change the fact that we didn't communicate for three weeks."

He frowned at her. "You're still not telling me what's going on," he said. "Spit it out."

She took a sip of her ice water, hoping the cool hydration would help calm her nerves. "What made you come to Chantaine?"

"You," he said.

She gave a nod, but didn't say anything.

"And I missed you," he admitted.

"That's good to know," she said in a dry voice.

"What the hell—" He broke off. "What's going on?"

"I'd rather not discuss it at the moment," she said. "I'd rather hear your true feelings for me."

He met her gaze for a long moment, then raked his hand through his hair. "You're more important to me than I had planned," he said.

"What had you planned?" she asked.

He shrugged. "I knew we would be together."

"So you planned for a fling, a temporary affair," she said.

"Yes."

His honest answer, which she'd asked for, stabbed at her.

"What had you planned?" he asked.

His question caught her off guard. "I don't know that I made any real plans," she said. "I just knew I couldn't turn away from you. The situation with your mother made it even more intense. I wanted to be with you. I wanted to be there for you." She closed her eyes and allowed the words to tumble from her heart. "I fell in love with you, and now I'm afraid I'm in this all by myself."

"You're not," he said. "But I don't want to be a wedge between you and your family. You would grow to hate me for that."

"It's not right for you to make that decision for me. Don't you see that in another way you're treating me like Stefan does? You're treating me like I don't know my own mind and heart." She clasped her hands together tightly and voiced her worst fear. "Are you sure this isn't some kind of smokescreen to hide the fact that you don't really love me and you don't want to be with me?"

His eyes lit with anger. "That's the most ridiculous thing I've ever heard you say."

"It isn't at all ridiculous to me, and it occurs to me that if I have to extract a commitment from you, then maybe I don't want it after all," she said, feeling a terrible wrenching sensation inside her.

He pulled her against him. "What do you want from me?"

"Not much," she said. "Just undying love, devotion and adoration."

"You've had that for months," he said.

She was afraid to believe him. "Why didn't you tell me?" she asked, her eyes burning with tears.

"I had to wait for you to catch up," he said and cupped her face.

Pippa finally saw everything she'd been afraid to wish for right there in his eyes.

"I love you, Pippa. I just don't want to make your life a living hell. I want to give you an opportunity to—" he shrugged "—come to your senses."

"Too late for that," she said, laughing breathlessly. "Besides, if being without you means I'm coming to my senses, then I don't want to do that." She bit her lip. "But there's something else I have to tell you."

"What?"

"I'm pregnant."

## *Epilogue*

Nic felt as if Pippa had hit him upside the head with a two-by-four. In a way, she had. It took three seconds before his mind moved into high gear. His immediate response was primitive and protective.

"You have to marry me," he said. "Your brother may want to kill me, but our child deserves a father."

Pippa winced. "That was romantic," she said in a wry voice.

Nic sweated bullets. He couldn't lose her. He had to protect her. He had to protect their child. He had to make her see everything he'd tried to hide. "I love you. I want to be with you all the time. Forever. I just didn't know how we could work it out with your family. Cut me some slack. I didn't plan on falling for a princess."

"That's much better," she said and pressed her face against his chest. "I wanted you to want me for me, not just because I'm having your child."

"That was never an issue," he said, stroking her crazy curls with his hand. He couldn't believe his luck. Pippa was pure gold without her title and somehow he'd managed to win her heart. "So am I gonna need to do the pirate thing and steal you away?"

She laughed and the husky sound vibrated against his chest. "No. I think everything will be okay once you talk with Stefan."

Nic anticipated a rough discussion, but was determined to do whatever was necessary for her and their baby. "I'm up for it."

"My family can be difficult," she said.

"You're worth it," he said and sealed his promise to her with a kiss.

Later that day, Nic met with Stefan. Nic didn't blame Stefan for being protective of Pippa. She was worth protecting. If the situation were reversed and Stefan had gotten his sister pregnant, Nic would have knocked him into next week. Nic admired Stefan's physical restraint and did everything he could to reassure the prince that he was devoted to Pippa. Nic suspected it would take a while to win over Pippa's clan, but he would keep chipping away at it.

Despite their differences, Nic and Stefan had a lot in common. One thing they both agreed on was that Nic and Pippa should get married right away. Three weeks later, he pledged everything including his troth, allegiance, love and devotion to Pippa. He was in it for good and he was relieved that she was, too. Nic hadn't known he could love a woman this much, but he'd never met anyone who brought him so much peace and happiness at the same time. He knew it wasn't possible to be any happier than he was with Pippa.

Until Pippa took him to a level he'd never imagined months later, when she gave birth to a beautiful baby girl. Pippa insisted that they name the baby Amelie and Nic had a feeling that the baby was gonna wrap him around her finger the same way her mother had. He was damn sure he didn't deserve all this joy, but he wasn't giving up the treasure he'd been given for anything. Her Highness was stuck with him, and thank God, she seemed to be just as happy about it as he was.

\* \* \* \* \*

# REQUEST YOUR FREE BOOKS!

## 2 FREE NOVELS PLUS 2 FREE GIFTS!

### ♦ Harlequin®

# SPECIAL EDITION

## Life, Love & Family

**YES!** Please send me 2 FREE Harlequin® Special Edition novels and my 2 FREE gifts (gifts are worth about $10). After receiving them, if I don't wish to receive any more books, I can return the shipping statement marked "cancel." If I don't cancel, I will receive 6 brand-new novels every month and be billed just $4.49 per book in the U.S. or $5.24 per book in Canada. That's a saving of at least 14% off the cover price! It's quite a bargain! Shipping and handling is just 50¢ per book in the U.S. and 75¢ per book in Canada.* I understand that accepting the 2 free books and gifts places me under no obligation to buy anything. I can always return a shipment and cancel at any time. Even if I never buy another book, the two free books and gifts are mine to keep forever.

235/335 HDN FEGF

Name _____ (PLEASE PRINT)

Address _____ Apt. #

City _____ State/Prov. _____ Zip/Postal Code

Signature (if under 18, a parent or guardian must sign)

### Mail to the **Reader Service**:
**IN U.S.A.:** P.O. Box 1867, Buffalo, NY  14240-1867
**IN CANADA:** P.O. Box 609, Fort Erie, Ontario  L2A 5X3

Not valid for current subscribers to Harlequin Special Edition books.

**Want to try two free books from another line?**
**Call 1-800-873-8635 or visit www.ReaderService.com.**

* Terms and prices subject to change without notice. Prices do not include applicable taxes. Sales tax applicable in N.Y. Canadian residents will be charged applicable taxes. Offer not valid in Quebec. This offer is limited to one order per household. All orders subject to credit approval. Credit or debit balances in a customer's account(s) may be offset by any other outstanding balance owed by or to the customer. Please allow 4 to 6 weeks for delivery. Offer available while quantities last.

**Your Privacy**—The Reader Service is committed to protecting your privacy. Our Privacy Policy is available online at www.ReaderService.com or upon request from the Reader Service.

We make a portion of our mailing list available to reputable third parties that offer products we believe may interest you. If you prefer that we not exchange your name with third parties, or if you wish to clarify or modify your communication preferences, please visit us at www.ReaderService.com/consumerschoice or write to us at Reader Service Preference Service, P.O. Box 9062, Buffalo, NY 14269. Include your complete name and address.

HSE11B

*Enjoy a month of compelling, emotional stories, including
a poignant new tale of love lost and found from*

# Sarah Mayberry

When Angela Bartlett loses her best friend to a rare heart
condition, it seems only natural that she step in and help
widower and friend Michael Young. The last thing she
expects is to find herself falling for him....

## Within Reach

*Available August 7!*

> "I loved it. I thought the story was very believable.
> The characters were endearing. The author wrote beautifully...
> I will be looking for future books by Sarah Mayberry."
> —Sherry, Harlequin® Superromance® reader, on *Her Best Friend*

Find more great stories this month from
Harlequin® Superromance® at

**www.Harlequin.com**

*Angie Bartlett and Michael Robinson are friends. And following the death of his wife, Angie's best friend, their bond has grown even more. But that's all there is…right?*

*Read on for an exciting excerpt of WITHIN REACH by Sarah Mayberry, available August 2012 from Harlequin® Superromance®.*

"HEY. RIGHT ON TIME," Michael said as he opened the door.

The first thing Angie registered was his fresh haircut and that he was clean shaven—a significant change from the last time she'd visited. Then her gaze dropped to his broad chest and the skintight black running pants molded to his muscular legs. The words died on her lips and she blinked, momentarily stunned by her acute awareness of him.

"You've cut your hair," she said stupidly.

"Yeah. Decided it was time to stop doing my caveman impersonation."

He gestured for her to enter. As she brushed past him she caught the scent of his spicy deodorant. He preceded her to the kitchen and her gaze traveled across his shoulders before dropping to his backside. Angie had always made a point of not noticing Michael's body. They were friends and she didn't want to know that kind of stuff. Now, however, she was forcibly reminded that he was a *very* attractive man.

Suddenly she didn't know where to look.

It was then that she noticed the other changes—the clean kitchen, the polished dining table and the living room free of clutter and abandoned clothes.

"Look at you go." Surely these efforts meant he was rejoining life.

He shrugged, but seemed pleased she'd noticed. "Getting there."

They maintained eye contact and the moment expanded. A connection that went beyond the boundaries of their friendship formed between them. Suddenly Angie wanted Michael in ways she'd never felt before. *Ever.*

"Okay. Let's get this show on the road," his six-year-old daughter, Eva, announced as she marched into the room.

Angie shook her head to break the spell and focused on Eva. "Great. Looking forward to a little light shopping?"

"Yes!" Eva gave a squeal of delight, then kissed her father goodbye.

Angie didn't feel 100 percent comfortable until she was sliding into the driver's seat.

Which was dumb. It was nothing. A stupid, odd bit of awareness that meant *nothing.* Michael was still Michael, even if he was gorgeous. Just because she'd tuned in to that fact for a few seconds didn't change anything.

*Does Angie's new awareness mark a permanent shift in their relationship? Find out in WITHIN REACH by Sarah Mayberry, available August 2012 from Harlequin® Superromance®.*

HSREXP0812